PARTNERS IN CRIME

Rachel Bowdler

CONTENT WARNINGS

Murder, death, blood, and violence

Mentions of familial problems such as neglectful parenting

ONE

"'Perhaps the most interesting thing about Herbert Humphrey's victims is that most of them were never found; and, had he not called in sick to work that day, Humphrey never would have been discovered at all.'"

Bryce read from the script with perfect ease, the black microphone bisecting her features down the middle. With her headphones on and eyes cast down, Thea knew everything else came secondary to her best friend now. She was in the zone. It was about the only time Thea managed to distract her from her usual problems, and she cherished each moment they spent recording down here, in the basement of her mother's bookstore, paying little heed to anything that existed outside of these dank four walls.

"With a name like Herbert Humphrey, maybe we should've expected a few dead bodies."

It was Thea's job to lighten the mood; to go off-script and improvise so that listeners of *Perfect Crimes*, their weekly independent true-crime podcast, wouldn't tire of their sinister subject matter too quickly. Not that Thea could imagine anyone tiring of such a thing. Serial killers were like snowflakes: each one had a unique shape, a different mindset and signature, a new way of leaving their victims behind. Herbert Humphrey's method just so happened to have been ditching the remains in Sal's Scrapyard, where he worked Monday to Friday in a quaint town only a few hours from Stone Grange, where Thea and Bryce both lived.

"Well, it's not all that difficult to envision a middle-aged man named Herbert as a little bit of a loner." Bryce nodded her agreement, though her audience couldn't see her. With the shoddy, second-hand recording equipment and the less than optimal — but actually quite apt — setting, it was easy to forget that people other than themselves *would* listen to this conversation. They'd been doing this for so long now that it felt like second nature to talk to each other through microphones, and almost a decade of friendship meant that Thea was comfortable enough around Bryce to slip into her stupid jokes and uninteresting facts. Perhaps *too* comfortable, she'd come to wonder recently.

"'Everybody in town claimed to have had some sort of strange run-in with him at one time or another,'" Bryce continued. "'Bad vibes, as Thea would say.'"

"'Serial killer vibes.'" Thea cast a small smirk Bryce's way. It was returned with the soft, dimpled swells of Bryce's wan cheeks; Thea's favorite sight. "'And indeed, the bad vibes came to fruition. On April 19th, 1999, we now know that Herbert Humphrey claimed his first victim, Judy Carlton. Two weeks later, his second, Simon Lowe. At the time, both of them were declared missing; their bodies never have been found. It was the third that led to Humphrey's downfall. On May 11th, 1999, a plain old Tuesday in the lazy town of Oakfold, our silly, silly man Humphrey called in sick with a virus.' A little strange, no?"

Though Thea was too busy reading her scrawled notes to lift her gaze, she could practically hear Bryce rolling her eyes across the table. "Here comes another of Thea's conspiracies. Maybe we should make a new series for them."

"Don't tempt me." Thea grinned. She'd toyed with the idea plenty of times, but Bryce refused to do it with her. After an infinite amount of puppy-dog eyes, begging, bribes involving extra cheesy fries and ice cream sundaes from Dina's Diner, Thea had finally given up trying. "But no, I don't know if I believe he was really sick. We all know that serial killers like to be recognized, famous even, in cases such as these ones. The victims held little connection to Humphrey, if any. They were just unfortunate souls who happened to be easy targets when the killer was ready to strike. So, it begs the question: if Humphrey went to so much work to hide the bodies in the scrapyard, why would he suddenly be careless enough to call in sick the morning after dumping his last victim?"

"Because he got too cocky. He thought he'd hid it well enough," Bryce answered, ever the logical one.

Thea wrinkled her nose. She didn't care much for logic. "No. I don't buy it. The thing is, there were rumors about the third and final victim. Apparently, Humphrey was seen around *a lot* with his last kill, a married mother of two named Laura Adams. Some people even suspected that they were having an affair while Laura's husband was out of town. Maybe the weight of what he'd done, killing the woman he loved, knocked him sick to his stomach, and that's why he took a day off. Maybe he *decided* to hang up his knife and end his spree after the last one got too much, too real."

"I think it would take more than a day to recover from the guilt of murdering your lover," Bryce countered.

Movement caught Thea's eye, distracting her from the argument. From his corner desk, Mikey gestured for them to wrap it up with winding fingers. They must have surpassed their forty-five minute mark.

Thea sighed, pressing her lips into a thin line. Tuesday mornings were her favorite day of the week. The basement distanced her from reality, from everything. In these short moments, it was just Bryce and Thea, talking, until everything felt simpler and easier to bear. She was always sad to see it come to an end.

It was also the only place she ever saw Bryce loosen up. Between working long shifts at the arcade six days a week and raising her sixteen-year-old sister, she had a lot on her shoulders. Thea liked knowing that this was the place where that weight could lessen slightly, and that she could be a part of the reason for it. It was the least Bryce deserved.

"Either way," Thea's fingers curled around her mic as she brought the episode to a close, "there's a lesson to be learned here, Bryce."

"And what's that?"

"Don't call in sick the day after you've dumped a body at your place of work."

"I'll keep it in mind should I ever decide to kill you."

Thea gasped, a hand pressed to her chest in feigned disgust. "You would never."

"You keep testing me," shrugged Bryce. "Stealing my fries, getting me up at seven every Sunday to help you with inventory, having me capture all the spiders in the basement. You're on thin ice."

It was true that Thea did those things. Bryce always got her own back, though, by scooping the jam out of Thea's donuts or forcing her to keep her company at the arcade on slow weekday afternoons. "You signed up for that when you became my best friend."

Bryce only hummed without commitment, glaring at Mikey, who reeled his fingers more aggressively now. "Well, that's all we have time for this week, you sick and twisted bunch. Make sure you set a reminder for next week's episode, where we'll be talking about an unsolved mystery involving a Jane Doe found drowned in a shallow lake. Thanks for listening."

"Goodbye, dear friends," Thea sang as she always did, and then Mikey cast them a thumbs up to let them know the recording had ended. Blowing out a breath, she slid the headphones off her sweaty ears and cracked her knuckles. "That was a fun one, I think."

Bryce winced at the sound and then glimpsed the time on her phone. "I better go. Gus wants me to open up today."

"Ugh, Gus." Thea scoffed at the mention of Bryce's demanding boss. Usually, Bryce at least had time for a cup of coffee and a browse through the bookstore before she left. "Milkshakes tonight to make up for it?"

With a pause that left her leather jacket suspended on only one arm, Bryce pondered the offer. "And burgers?"

"Ooh, good call. I want double cheese and bacon."

"Who, me?" Mikey muttered under his breath as he clicked away at his laptop. "Oh, no. I'm busy. Thanks for the invite, though."

"Oh, Mikey." Thea ruffled her friend's dark hair until it loosened from its top knot. "You're always welcome to hang out with us."

With a huff of annoyance, he swatted her away. "Uh huh."

"No he's not," replied Bryce bluntly. "He gets bored of us after five minutes and pulls out his earphones."

"'Bored *with*,'" he corrected. "And you talk about womanly stuff, like... menstrual cycles and *Dirty Dancing*."

Both of them snorted at that. Thea and Bryce rarely watched rom-coms together, though they might've occasionally been guilty of the former, and refused to censor their monthly pain for the sake of a man. Naturally, their movie nights almost *always* ended up with a marathon of Wes Craven films.

"*Please*," Thea said, pained. "*You* talk about *Dirty Dancing*. We talk about *A Nightmare on Elm Street*. Just say you're afraid of Freddie Krueger and go."

"Every sane person is afraid of Freddie Krueger." Mikey kicked his feet into the spare chair opposite and linked his hands across his soft stomach. "That dude traumatized me for life. Anyway, I have a favor to ask you both."

"Nope. Can't. Busy," said Bryce.

"You don't even know what it is yet!"

"Make it quick." Bryce was ready to dash off, her purse tucked under one shoulder and the button of her purple shirt buttoned to the top, now. The compulsory bow tie was scrunched in her hand, Bryce's least favorite part of the uniform. It just so happened to be Thea's favorite, not because the white and grey stripes were silly, but because Thea actually quite liked bow ties. And bow ties on women...

"I need you... I was wondering..."

"This is why *we* do the talking and you do the other stuff," Thea huffed.

Mikey sighed in frustration. "The thing is... I like this girl. You probably know her. She works in that cool goth place down the street. Leather 'n' Lace."

Bryce snapped her fingers. "Oh, you mean 'Adult Wednesday Addams!'"

"So... 'Morticia Addams,'" Thea teased.

5

"Her name is *Hannah*," Mikey ground out, "and I like her, okay? I've been trying to find an excuse to talk to her for weeks. In fact, I have a grand total of ten rose quartz crystals and five Green Day pins to show for my failed attempts. Everytime I go into the store, I freeze up."

"I've seen her lining up outside that new cocktail bar on Friday nights after work," Bryce shrugged. "Maybe you should do whatever it is people do nowadays. Dance or grind or whatever." Bryce often talked as though she was decades older than them, and not a very baby-faced twenty-six. Most likely a result of becoming a second mother to her younger sister, Olivia.

"Exactly. That's where you two would have to come in."

"Gross," Thea gagged. "I'm not grinding on you."

"Oh. My. God." Mikey's eyes drifted to the cobwebbed ceiling as though he was pleading with a higher being to send down reinforcements, or at least give him strength to make it through the conversation. "I'm asking you to be my wingwomen."

Both Thea's and Bryce's features crumpled with frowns.

"I think you should ask your men friends for that," said Thea. "When women see other women around men, they tend to assume at least one of them is a girlfriend, and I truly do not wish that label upon myself or Bryce."

"Forget it." Mikey punched something into his keyboard angrily, and it left a shred of guilt in Thea's gut. She knew that other than the two of them, Mikey kept to himself. He probably didn't have any other friends in town to help him out, and despite the work he did for the podcast, he rarely asked for favors in return.

"All right," she sighed, eliciting a daggered glare from Bryce. "The Bloody Mary, Friday, nine."

"Ugh." Bryce groaned her disapproval, but it was clear she didn't have time to back out now. Mikey, on the other hand, looked ready either to cheer or jump with joy, and Thea shot him a warning glare before he got the chance.

"I'll be upstairs if you need me," Thea told him, though he knew by now where to find her during the day and always ended up providing good excuses for her to sneak away from the store.

She followed a heavy-footed Bryce up the narrow, creaking stairs, worried eyes boring into her back. As they reached the top, she begged, "Don't be in a mood with me, Bryce."

Bryce was panting slightly as they came to a stop, and rested to catch her breath against a stack of boxes along the back wall. The others were covered in shelves brimming with untidy piles of colorful books gathering dust. It instantly made Thea's nose itch, and she fought back a sneeze as Bryce replied.

"I'm not in a mood with you. I just have better things to be doing than playing Cupid for Mikey. He'll have a new crush next week anyway."

"Oh, come *on.* We never do anything fun anymore. It'll make a change from my mother's basement or the diner, won't it?"

"And what about Liv?"

"Liv is almost seventeen," Thea reminded. "She doesn't need to be babysat *every* night."

A muscle feathered in Bryce's jaw. So stubborn. It left Thea sad that she had to work so hard to convince her best friend that she deserved just one night of fun.

"Do I need to sing 'the Piña Colada Song?'" She poked Bryce lightly in the ribs. "Come on, Bryce. *One* night. It'll be good for you."

"Ugh," Bryce caved, and Thea knew it was only to shut her up. *"Fine."*

With a proud grin, Thea tapped the upturned peak of Bryce's nose, a habit from high school she still refused to break. "Yay! Bryce and Thea's night on the town. Maybe we could make it into a monthly podcast."

"No." Bryce pushed through the door and strutted through the store without a second glance. Thea followed with more than a little excitement whirling in her stomach. She would be happy spending any sort of time with Bryce, but it had been so long since they'd let loose and done something different.

She was going to say as much when a tall figure caught her eye. An unfamiliar man dressed in a long, black trench coat stood at the cash register, talking to Thea's mother, Nina Curtis. Breath hitching, Thea reached out and pinched Bryce's elbow to stop her from going any further, and slid behind the nearest row of bookshelves before peeking her head out unnoticed.

The man was pale, grey-haired, with a raspy voice that set Thea's teeth on edge. From here, she couldn't make out what they spoke about, but the pile of books in front of him all bore 'James Patterson' on their spines, in that ridiculously large font three times larger than their title. *Real subtle.*

"What are you doing?" hissed Bryce.

As Thea shushed her, she got a subtle waft of Bryce's coco-nutty deodorant. "Serial killer vibes," she whispered, pointing an accusatory finger towards the man.

"Why are you like this?" Bryce tutted and straightened up. "You can't just go around accusing people of having 'serial killer vibes', Thea. I'm going to work."

"See you tonight, then!" called Thea, stepping nonchalantly away from the shelves she'd been hiding behind as Bryce exchanged goodbyes with Thea's mother.

"Thea," Nina summoned her from behind the counter, wearing her best customer service smile as she gestured her daughter over. "Come meet our new neighbor, Mr. Godfrey."

"Just John is fine." The scrawny middle-aged man offered his hand, and Thea shook it while trying not to grimace at just how cold and clammy it was.

"It's nice to meet you."

"And you. I have a daughter not too much younger than you, actually. She's away, studying at Whitman, though."

"Thea applied to Whitman!" Nina felt it necessary to add, as though applying to an esteemed, low acceptance rate college was just as much an accomplishment as actually getting into one. Needless to say, Whitman College had not wanted Thea's horrifyingly average grades sullying their fancy, private halls, and she'd ended up staying closer to home to study criminology at Washington State, a qualification she had little use for now, though she'd enjoyed the earning of it enough.

Thea didn't *want* to pursue any of the traditional careers

associated with her field. She wanted to do what she did now, but on a larger scale: document and report on true crime, try to understand why it happened and how, and perhaps even one day write mystery and thriller novels based on her endless hours of research. Her mother was none too happy about wasting a hefty amount of money on her education only for Thea to sit in her basement and record podcasts, but the series was at least taking off and finally reaching people well outside of their dreary little town.

"It's a lovely place," nodded John. "I should get going, anyway, but feel free to drop by sometime. I'm just around the corner."

"I'll have Thea send over a lasagna!" Nina waved pleasantly, though Thea could not remember agreeing to such a thing. With a resigned sigh, she plucked her apron from under the counter and tied it around her waist in a tight bow before picking up the Stephen King novel she was midway through. It was rarely busy in the mornings, and Thea had plenty of time to kill.

In fact, that was the only thing she ever seemed to do: kill time. She was getting quite bored of it.

✳ ✳ ✳

The clattering of the coin-pushing machines spitting out tarnished quarters was giving Bryce a headache. The fact that she was currently suffocating in the Albert the Albatross mascot costume her boss had forced upon her didn't help. In the musty, ripe-smelling opening of the beak, sweat poured down her face. She could barely see the notes she was supposed to be exchanging for coins for the waiting customer, and with the foam yellow gloves she didn't even think were anatomically possible for the seabird she was dressed as, sorting it was even more difficult.

Somehow, she managed it.

"Thank you for visiting Albatross Arcades," she rattled off to the old woman, who'd been frowning at her impatiently the entire time. "I hope you have a squawking good time!"

The costume was supposed to be worn to entertain the kids, so why Bryce had been wearing it since noon on a school day she didn't know. It wasn't even supposed to be her turn, but somehow, Peter had wriggled his way out of the responsibility today. Asthma, he'd claimed. Bryce would make sure he had far worse than asthma wrong with him if he made her wear it again this week.

Thankfully, the quick peek she took at her phone behind the counter told her it was almost eight, which meant her shift was due for finishing. She'd need at least three showers to wash away whatever germs were incubating in the polyester. It made her shudder just to think of it.

Bryce *hated* working here. She hated how her fingers felt grimy after touching other people's coins and tokens all day. She hated the constant, high-pitched theme music of the Pac-Man machine, which rang through her head long after her day was done. She hated the smell of processed meat wafting from the hot dog vendor, and the rowdy kids who found tormenting Bryce far more entertaining than the hundreds of games they came in to play. She hated her boss, who never let her take time off work and always kept her past the end of her shift. She hated that when she went home, microwave meals had been set out by her sister because Bryce was too exhausted and late to cook a decent meal for her. But Bryce had applied for dozens of other jobs and had been successful in none. Stone Grange was a dying little town with not much in it save for the shopping street and weekend markets, and the places that *were* hiring wanted qualifications Bryce had never been able to get. She was trapped with no way out, and the day-in-day-out grind was slowly killing her.

"Excuse me, Albert."

Bryce had to lean over the desk to find the source of the voice, a little boy missing his two front teeth, probably because the rest of his face was stained with the bright blue dye of sour candy.

"Hello." Bryce flapped her wings, wondering if perhaps she should take up a career in acting. "Are you having a squawking good time?"

"Yes." The boy laughed and held out a stack of tickets. "How many for cotton candy?"

Technically, the tickets were supposed to be read in a machine, with the total printed off to exchange for prizes, but Bryce didn't feel like explaining that to a sugar-drunk six-year-old, so she counted them out by hand. He was a few dozen short, but she plucked him a bag of candy floss from the display behind her anyway, the pink fluff shrunken slightly after a day of sweating in humid, early summer heat. Just how Bryce felt. Shrunken and shrivelled. "Here you go. Don't eat it all at once."

"Thank you, Albert!" The boy grinned and then ran back to his parents on the other side of the arcade. Bryce sighed, if only to circulate some air in her costume, glad when Peter wandered over with a fresh bag of quarters and tokens.

"I won't tell Gus you got off early if you don't," he smirked, joining her behind the desk. The coins spilled into the cash register, only worsening the throbbing in Bryce's temples.

"Really?"

"I owe you one," Peter said. "Besides, I just saw your friend come in. Thea, right?"

"Right." If she hadn't been running the risk of exposing the fact that Albert the Albatross was actually a twenty-six-year-old woman in a costume to a bunch of kids, she would've ripped herself out of the mascot then and there.

"Hey, I've been meaning to ask you something," Peter continued, casting Bryce a sidelong glance.

"Make it quick."

Bryce caught sight of Thea weaving in and out of families to find her. She waved a gloved hand to make it known that she wasn't in her usual get-up tonight.

"Well... Okay. I..." Bryce had found out an hour into her first ever shift that Peter Keane talked an awful lot about nothing at all. She was used to his half-formed rambling by now, but it seemed to drag on even longer tonight.

"You...?" she urged.

He scratched at the peach fuzz on his chin. Though older

than her, his fair whiskers had never thickened to a beard, but he seemed to wear the sparse facial hair with pride all the same. "It's just... I was wondering... There's this Thai place on Hoover Street I like."

Bryce frowned. "Okay... That's not a question."

"I'm asking," Peter sucked in a deep breath that expanded all the way from his chest to his stomach, "if you would like to maybe go eat Thai food with me on Hoover Street. Or any street. Any place. Anywhere."

"Bryce doesn't like Thai food, buddy," Thea piped up as she finally reached them — and thank God. She'd saved Bryce from perhaps the most uncomfortable date proposal she'd ever heard.

"Oh..." Peter's face crumpled in disappointment. "Well, what about pizza?"

"Sure, pizza," said Thea. "We'd love to."

"Actually, I was asking Bryce —"

"Why don't we talk about this tomorrow, Peter?" Bryce interjected quickly. And then, it seemed her family and friends were all on her side tonight, because a familiar, dark set of space buns popped up from behind the air hockey table.

Olivia rarely came to Bryce's place of work, even with her friends, so worry gnawed at Bryce as soon as she saw her. She left both Thea and Peter forgotten at the desk, tail feathers colliding with almost every machine on her way through the arcade. "Hey. What's up?"

"Shh," Liv shushed, pulling Bryce aside by the wing and ducking beneath a pinball machine. "My friends are over there."

"Oh, I see. You're embarrassed that your sister is Albert the Albatross," Bryce nodded, and then, for good measure, began to squawk and flap her wings. "Hello, Olivia! *Squawk!* How was — *squawk!* — school?"

Liv glared through eyes not too dissimilar from Bryce's own. They were the same shade of molten brown, framed by the same thick lashes inherited from their absentee father, whom they'd both decided long ago that they despised, and wanted nothing more to do with. "I hate you so much."

"I know," Bryce sang. "What's up?"

"I only came to ask you if I could go to a party tonight. It's Tasha's birthday, and everyone from school's going —"

Bryce lifted a hand to interrupt. "Who the hell has parties on a Tuesday?"

"Oh, come on. This isn't the Eighties anymore." With a pointed look, Liv crossed her arms over her chest. She wore one of Bryce's old Nirvana T-shirts, which were apparently more fashionable now than when Bryce had bought it as a wannabe edgy teenager and, as a consequence, had been mocked to no end. "People throw parties on any day they want to now."

"I hadn't even been *born* in the Eighties," scoffed Bryce, only slightly offended that an extra decade had been added to her age. She sure *felt* over thirty these days, if not older. "And the answer is no. It's a school night."

"Oh, come on!" Liv whined as though she was a three-year-old about to throw a tantrum. "Everyone's going!"

"That's because everyone probably lies to their parental guardians. You are one of the good ones." Bryce ruffled her sister's hair, leaving it to stick up in flyaway strands.

Liv only glared. "So if I want to go to a party, I should just … not ask you?"

Jaw clenching, Bryce cocked her head and hoped the daggers she threw were visible beneath the albatross mascot's curved beak. "Don't test me."

"I'll be home by twelve?" tried Liv anyway.

A loud guffaw that probably sounded more like a real squawk than any other she'd attempted today emerged from the mask. "Nice try."

"Eleven?"

"Ten-thirty." Liv was about as independent as Bryce was, and trying to get her to stay in now would only leave them arguing here all night. Bryce didn't have the energy for that. "No drinking. No drugs. How are you getting home?"

"She lives two blocks away. I'll walk."

"Not on your own you won't."

"Then I'll get a cab."

The idea made Bryce uneasy, but she knew she would have to let Liv... well, *live*, someday. Besides, Stone Grange was about the most harmless town in the entire state of Washington. She'd done far worse things than her sister at that age and been... fine... *mostly.* "You'll text me when you set off home."

"I will," Liv agreed.

"It wasn't a question. Is your phone charged?"

"Yep."

Warily, Bryce sighed. "All right. I'll see you tonight. *Ten-thirty* or else."

"Got it." Liv was already walking away — taking a scenic route around the kids' rides, so as not to be seen anywhere near Bryce in front of her friends. Apparently, standing beside Thomas the Tank Engine was less embarrassing than Albert.

Bryce rolled her eyes. She loved her sister. If she didn't, she wouldn't have been working her ass off here everyday, miserable, to make sure they had enough food and Liv enough savings in her account to go off to college — which, so far, was proving difficult. Even so, it was testing at times. Bryce didn't have a maternal bone in her body, but taking care of Liv had never been a choice.

Their mother had left nine years ago, and there had been no one else to take care of things but her. She'd turned eighteen and registered as Liv's official guardian before the social workers came knocking. Bryce had worked ever since to make sure Liv never felt as though she was lacking anything, not that their mother had left a lot to miss in the first place, unstable and cold as she'd been to them both. She'd cared more about drinking and whichever man was crawling into her bed that week.

It terrified her, though, that Bryce could mess up just as easily. That Liv might end up even worse off than Bryce had been at her age, if Bryce didn't get things right. She only wanted to give her sister the life *she* hadn't been able to have. College, a job she enjoyed, that would give her enough money that she never had to go without. It was hard work. Harder now that Liv was ready to stand on her own two feet and fly away.

Before Bryce could worry too much about it, she went back to the desk. "I'll be right out," she told Thea before disappearing into the back rooms, where the staff took their breaks. In all the time she'd been here, she'd never been given a lock for her locker, and could only hope every time she came in that her purse hadn't been stolen. Luck had served her well so far.

She hauled off the hat and costume with a deep sigh of relief, the cool air hitting the sheen of sweat caking her skin. Thank God the day was over. She was ready for an extra large, extra chocolatey milkshake.

* * *

"I talked to the new neighbor guy from the bookstore after you left this morning," Thea informed Bryce after they'd slid into the only vacant booth in Dina's Diner. A storm had just broken through the humidity, and it seemed half the town was taking shelter here. The rain pelted against the window, Dina's neon-pink sign leaving an eerie glow reflected on the wet asphalt of the parking lot. Thea was glad to be out of it, with the speckled sheet of glass to protect her from the sporadic bouts of thunder and lightning.

"Hmm?" Bryce hummed distractedly, tongue poking out in concentration as she peeled the pickles from her burger.

Thea tutted in disgust and pinched them off her plate. "Monster." Eight years of friendship had not made her any more comfortable with the fact that Bryce hated pickles, and she said as much each time they ate together.

Usually, Bryce would make some clever retort that Thea never would've been able to expect, but tonight, she remained as glum as the weather outside. Instead of tucking into her burger — double cheese and bacon as promised — she dragged a wilted fry around her plate, leaving a trail of ketchup in its wake.

"Bryce? You okay?"

"Yeah." Bryce lifted her gaze and blinked the solemn trance

away. "What happened with the guy?"

"His name is John Godfrey. He has a daughter around our age studying at Whitman."

"Fancy."

Thea nodded her agreement, but her brows furrowed. She still couldn't quite get Bryce to lock eyes with her, and it left her unsettled, reaching desperately in an attempt to catch her. "What did your sister say at the arcade earlier?"

Bryce waved her hand dismissively. "Some party. I told her she could go, but now I don't think I should have."

"You know if you didn't let her, she'd probably sneak out anyway."

"No." Defeated, she shoved the tray of food away and focused on her milkshake instead. "She's not like me."

"Exactly," Thea pointed out, sliding the tray back in an attempt to get her to eat. "She's better. You have nothing to worry about."

"I'll try not to take offense to that."

The milkshake slurped and gurgled through Bryce's striped straw. Thea tried not to notice the way her lips puckered, or the way the raindrops on the window dappled her golden complexion with shadows. Thea had been doing that a lot, lately; trying and failing not to notice things about Bryce. It was as though one day, she'd been so certain she knew her best friend inside and out that she no longer *really* looked at her anymore, and then the next, out of nowhere, she'd started noticing *everything* about Bryce, every beauty spot and every wrinkle that formed when she smiled or frowned or laughed. It had taken Thea so aback that her breath would hitch and her heart would stutter each time it happened. It made her feel weird. Fuzzy and feverish and weird. She'd discovered that she was pansexual years ago, now — and with Bryce's help, no less, since she'd been confident in her own bisexuality since adolescence — but it had still thrown her off. Best friends were off limits. She shouldn't think of Bryce that way.

But no matter how many bricks she stacked in an attempt to block that irritating part of her brain away from their perfect, uncomplicated friendship, it kept seeping through the cracks.

"You know I don't mean it that way. I mean she's better *behaved.*" Thea wriggled and shifted her gaze away so that she wouldn't have to listen to her pounding heart again. "*She's* not going to drink too many wine coolers and throw up on the neighbor's cat."

"*I* did that one time." Bryce glared.

"Well, I think one time is more than enough, don't you?" A smirk played on Thea's lips, but Bryce didn't return it, so she did all she could think of. She reached across the table and took Bryce's hand. It was cool from holding the milkshake and as soft as the rest of her. Thea had always loved playing with her fingers; they glittered with a myriad of jewelry and her nails always wore chipped black polish. It was a habit she'd never really broken, reaching for Bryce's hand when they watched a movie or as she drove Thea home. Bryce had never said anything about it; had always just let her.

But Thea wasn't doing this for her own comfort, now. She was trying desperately to tell Bryce it was okay. Everything was okay. She was here. So she squeezed her reassurance gently and didn't move or pull away.

"Bryce. Every sixteen-year-old goes to parties. I bet Liv will be the most sensible one there."

"I just worry," Bryce admitted, biting down on her lip. "I worry I'm doing it all wrong. If I keep her locked inside the house, I'm the strict, awful parent who doesn't let their kid do their own thing, and that will just make her lie to me. If I let her go, I'm... I'm like *her,* right?"

Her mother. Connie had been a lousy parent to both her girls. Bryce had raised herself, and not without struggle, and then had raised Liv, too, while Connie performed intermittent disappearing acts that had gradually increased in duration; her returns home had tapered off until one day, they'd just never seen her again, just like their father.

When Thea had first met Bryce, she'd smoked and partied, had shadows in her eyes that she was too young to have, because Connie hadn't cared enough. She'd let her do whatever she wanted, and set an example no young person should have witnessed. It made Thea ache to think of how lonely that must've been for her. Thea's own mother was a pain in the ass, but she at least gave a damn even now, when Thea was old enough that she no longer needed her to lean on.

"No," Thea whispered gently, and rose to round the booth so that she was closer to Bryce. Bryce shuffled down with reluctance, looking anywhere but at Thea. Thea knew just how much she hated to be vulnerable. It happened so rarely now. "You're *nothing* like her. You *know* that. *Liv* knows that. Because you *care.* Because you will *never* let Liv feel abandoned or alone. You have to start trusting her, though… and start trusting yourself that you've done a good enough job."

Bryce nodded and let Thea weave a finger delicately through her dark ponytail, bowing her head and steepling her fingers. "She keeps talking about college. I don't know if I can even afford it."

"She's a bright kid. There'll be scholarships." Thunder rumbled outside, but Thea barely noticed it, sitting here. Every ounce of her attention was on Bryce.

"Yeah." Bryce didn't sound all that convinced, but her eyes shone at least a little bit brighter, two pools of dark, wet ink against the fluorescents. Thea wished more than anything she could tell Bryce she didn't have to worry anymore. She wanted so badly to take away all of those troubles. It made her feel like a spoiled brat in comparison. She still rented the apartment above the bookstore from her mother and worked for her to pay for it. She'd never had to go out and look for a minimum wage job she had no interest in just to pay the bills. She'd never known what it was like to struggle at all; not financially, at least. She had what she needed to be comfortable, and would always have that to fall back on. Bryce deserved that luxury, too.

Hopeless and lost, Thea could only attempt to lighten the mood. "Maybe we'll win the lottery or the podcast will go viral overnight."

Bryce let a small grin curl across her lips at that. "Maybe."

Satisfied, Thea returned across the table to her burger. "It's going to be okay, Bryce. Promise."

"I know," she replied, voice so soft, so brittle, it sounded like it might break.

"Anyway, when are we going to talk about Peter asking you on a date?" An awful twinge of jealousy had shot through Thea's stomach when she'd overheard Peter Keane asking Bryce out in the arcade, though Bryce hadn't even said yes. Then again, she hadn't said no, either.

"Ugh," groaned Bryce. "Never. Thanks for saving me, by the way."

"You don't... *like* him?" Thea felt like a pathetic child in need of validation, reassurance. Not because *Thea* wanted to date Bryce instead (*are you sure?* a voice crooned inside her head), but because a new relationship might break their whole, wonderful dynamic. They'd only faced it once before, when Thea had entertained a musician in college. It hadn't ended well, and she knew Bryce had felt abandoned when Thea spent so much time away from home; away from her. Thea couldn't imagine having the situation reversed.

Bryce scoffed, now, finally taking a bite of her burger. Shreds of lettuce fell out of the bottom, and then a slice of tomato with it, but she seemed not to notice. "And when do I have time to date, Thea?"

That wasn't what Thea had asked. Was she avoiding the question? *Did* she like him? The thought sent panic roiling through her. "That's not an answer."

"No." Bryce rolled her eyes, exasperated. "Of course I don't *like* Peter. I have no interest in dating him *or* anyone else."

The relief felt as though Thea had sunk into a warm bubble bath, and she relaxed in her chair, the leather covers sticking to the backs of her thighs. Still, something ate at her for a reason she didn't want to acknowledge. *Or anyone else.* As though somehow, Thea herself had been rejected by the statement, too. "I don't think we're doing this whole twenties thing right. At this rate, we'll be single forever."

"Good," said Bryce through a mouthful of mustard. Again, that disappointment rattled through Thea in response. "It's easier that way."

Thea wished that wasn't the truth. She wished that she could find someone who slot into her life perfectly and set her on fire at the same time.

The problem was, she already had that, with the one person she wasn't supposed to. With Bryce.

TWO

Bryce was less than happy to be summoned to the bookstore at ten a.m.on the only day off she could afford to take that week. Why Thea couldn't have just waited for their scheduled lunch later that day, she didn't know, but she waved at Nina on her way to the bookstore's stockroom and trampled down the basement's loosely carpeted stairs with a huff. She was wearing her favorite boots: the black ones with the three-inch heels, and just *knew* she'd break her neck going down here one of these days.

Thea waited at the bottom, tapping her foot impatiently. The desk where they recorded the podcast episodes was still scattered with equipment and papers, but there was no sign of Mikey here.

"You called?" Bryce asked expectantly as she reached the final step, resting against the bannister as she regained her breath.

"An hour ago," said Thea stonily.

Bryce had barely been awake an hour ago when she'd gotten the call. She glared sourly to make the inconvenience known and mirrored Thea's defensive stance. "Excuse me for not rushing to answer your every beck and call."

"You're excused." Thea relaxed as though there hadn't been an issue to begin with and then picked up a thick newspaper from the desk. "In the future, when I say it's an emergency, it means *get over here now.*"

With a roll of her eyes, Bryce scoffed. She'd witnessed plenty of Thea's *emergencies* over the years: the time Thea had been stung by a wasp, for example, or the time she'd thought she'd seen Skeet Ulrich in the bookstore and it had turned out to be just Tommy, the guy who busked outside of the arcade seven days a week with a harmonica and acoustic guitar — otherwise known as the bane of Bryce's existence, what with all the Fray songs he loved to make even *more* whiny and pathetic. "Sure. It's not like I have a life of my own."

She didn't, really. Other than work, taking care of her sister, and the podcast, Bryce spent any spare time she could find watching *Friends* reruns and browsing through Media City job listings she wasn't qualified to apply for; it wasn't a city at all but Stone Grange's closest rundown lot of small TV studios. Still, spare time came rarely these days, and Thea *knew* that.

But she didn't seem to care, and when she finally handed the newspaper to Bryce, Bryce understood why.

'**Policeman Found Dead In Stone Grange Sewage System Three Days After Disappearance**,' the front page headline read in jarringly bold letters. Below it was a picture of a face she knew well:.Stone Grange's only decent cop, Isaac Harmer. An old archive photo had been used; the beaming smile on Harmer's face as he stood cradling some sort of award completely incongruous with the morbid black and white article. Bryce saw that friendly smile and remembered the time she'd gotten lost in Rosie's Garden Centre, when her mother had taken home the five goldfish she'd bought on a whim from the aquatics department but had completely forgotten about her daughter. Officer Harmer had held Bryce's hand until Connie finally returned for her an hour later. And then, when she'd been older and testing the boundaries of her alcohol tolerance with way too many shots of vodka, Harmer had found her puking on the side of the curb; he'd walked her home because she was too nauseous to get into his cop car. He hadn't even reported her for underage drinking. He'd just... wanted to make sure she was okay.

When rumors of his disappearance had spread through town a couple of days ago, Bryce had thought nothing of it. Isaac Harmer was the most reliable man in town. You could always find him wandering around, guiding elderly ladies across the street or having civil conversations with the raucous teens leaving smashed beer bottles in the local parks. If he wasn't around, it probably meant he was on vacation, she'd thought.

But Isaac hadn't been on vacation. He was gone.

Bryce's eyes stung and she couldn't make any sense of the words on the page. She threw the newspaper down, feeling as hollowed out as she had been on that day as a lost six-year-old without a family.

When she hadn't mattered to her mom, she'd mattered to Isaac Harmer. And Isaac was gone.

"I don't understand."

"Read it," Thea insisted, pushing the newspaper into Bryce's chest again.

Bryce thrust it away. She knew well enough what happened when bodies were dumped into sewers. They'd covered a similar cold case in the podcast just last week that had made even her grimace to talk about. No one had ever found *that* murderer's true identity.

"I don't want to. Just... just tell me why I'm here."

Thea lifted her brows and punched a pastel pink fingernail into the last sentence of the article, where one word showed clearly enough. *Homicide*. "It was a *murder,* Bryce. Isaac was murdered."

Bryce noticed the way Thea's eyes glittered at that, as if it was a good thing. As if they should be celebrating. It made nausea roil in Bryce's gut. She couldn't speak, couldn't think.

"Bryce," Thea whispered. "We have our very own Stone Grange murder. Do you have any idea what this will do for our podcast?"

"Our *podcast*?" The question was high-pitched with disbelief. "*A man is dead,* Thea. A *good* man, one I respected! And you're thinking about the *podcast*?"

"No." Thea softened, inching closer to Bryce. "No, I'm sorry, I'm not trying to be insensitive. But this is what we do, right? This is everything that *Perfect Crimes* is about."

"It's a little different when the dead guy is a man who pulled out a loose tooth for you when you were five."

"I know."

But Thea couldn't have known. She couldn't have known at all. Bryce was into murder and crime as much as any horror movie fanatic, but *Thea*... she was beginning to wonder if Thea was *too* into it.

"Look, if you don't want to talk about this anymore, we won't —"

"I don't," Bryce said, and was ignored.

"But *I* just think it's a little suspicious that this weird new family gets into town and then someone is found dead not that long after."

Bryce could only sigh in frustration. "Tell me you're not going to do this."

"*I* just think," Thea continued, making it known that she was, in fact, going to do this, "that if anyone should do a little freelance investigating, it's us, y'know? The case is ongoing and apparently they have no leads." She lifted her hand as though she was a fourth grader volunteering an answer in class. "*I* have a lead."

"*You* have a *theory*. One with absolutely no evidence to back it up. You can't just go accusing people of murder because they're new in town."

Thea shrugged. "I'm not accusing anyone of anything. But if it so happens that my mom made a lasagna for the Godfreys that she wants *me* to take over later... well, I can't help that, can I?"

Groaning, Bryce collapsed into the swivel chair, so well-used by now that it had a permanent ass print sunken into the padding. "Don't do this, Thea. Please."

"Do what?" An innocent smile crept onto Thea's pink lips. "I'm merely being a good neighbor."

"I won't be part of it. I liked Isaac. He was kind to me when..." *When I needed kindness*, Bryce wanted to say, but couldn't bring herself to, through the lump in her throat. It did make her sick, though, to think that somebody had ended his life and dumped him in the rotten sewers that ran beneath town. He deserved so much better than that.

"Fine," Thea shrugged. "I'll have Mikey carry the brownies, then."

It was clear Thea intended to do no such thing. She was baiting Bryce, knowing that for all her grief, she couldn't resist the chaos Thea always brought to their friendship. And perhaps the Godfreys *were* a little suspicious. And perhaps she didn't want Isaac Harmer's murder to go unpunished.

Perhaps that's why, with a long, jagged exhale of breath, she agreed. *"Fine.* I'll carry the damn brownies. But that's as far as this goes."

"As far as it goes." Thea extended her pinky finger in promise. Bryce curled her own around it knowing full well it would probably be broken. Maybe that's just what friendship was: a pile of broken promises.

* * *

"Yoohoo, Mr. Godfrey!" Thea waved over the white picket fence of the Godfreys' back yard, wondering what sort of job John must have if he could afford the large, three-story house beside the town's library and still be at home at one-thirty on a weekday.

She stopped in her tracks when she heard the crack of a spade burrow itself into damp, gravelly soil.

"Oh my God. He's burying a body," she whispered to Bryce.

Bryce rolled her eyes, clutching the Tupperware box of brownies in her hands.

John's gray head rose above the pointed wooden slats — which, Thea noted, could easily be used to impale somebody — as the sound of digging ceased. "Oh, hello. Thea, was it?"

"This is the guy you think is a killer?" Bryce muttered, lips downturned in disapproval. "He's wearing *linen."*

Thea clucked her tongue. "Have I taught you nothing? It's always the least suspicious ones." She neglected to mention the fact that John had appeared more suspicious in the bookstore a few days ago. Apparently, in the comfort of his own yard, he swapped his long black coat for light, well-ironed trousers and loose beige shirts.

Louder, she called to John, "Yep, Thea! My mom sent round some homemade lasagna and brownies."

"Ah!" Pale slices of color shifted across the slatted fence and John ambled to the gate, and then the bolts clicked and it creaked open on rusted hinges. "That's so kind of you both. And who is your friend?"

Bryce's silence made it very clear she had no intention of introducing herself, so Thea said, "This is my best friend, Bryce."

"Well, both of you do come in. We're in the process of digging out a fire pit and having a housewarming barbecue." He motioned to the uprooted patch of earth, the spade still thrust in the center. There was no corpse, Thea noted. Just a fire pit, as John had said. The serial killer vibes were dwindling awfully quickly. "It's a little early, I know, but you see, my daughter — "

A shrill peal of yaps broke through his words, the source a ball of white fluff rolling across the freshly-trimmed grass. There must be a dog somewhere in all that fur, Thea thought, with an arched eyebrow.

She didn't miss the way Bryce snorted as though to say 'I told you so'.

"Might I introduce you to Sugarplum?" John picked up the heap of white curls, sticking out his chin when a pink tongue swiped across his cheek. "She's very friendly. Loud, though."

"Sugarplum," Bryce repeated, reaching out to stroke the dog with an amused smirk. She cast Thea a pointed look. "What a *lovely* name."

Thea knew what she was trying to say: what a pretty, completely non-serial killer-ish thing to name a dog.

So perhaps John did not appear quite as dark and shadowy as he had in the bookstore. There *still* had been a murder in town right after he'd moved in, and he clearly liked his crime novels. It surely couldn't be a coincidence.

She shot Bryce a glare and placed the piled tupperware on a frosted glass patio table.

"*I* didn't name her," John said, as he fussed over his pet. "That was all Heidi."

"Who's Heidi?" inquired Thea, as nonchalantly as she could.

"That would be me," a musical voice sounded behind her, drawing her attention away from John and the dog. A younger woman made her way down the steps in flip-flops and a floral summer dress, the hem floating out behind her. Her hair was a tangle of ashy curls, cheeks well-chiseled and chin dimpled. She might've been the most beautiful girl Thea had ever seen, and she tried to keep her mouth from gaping open involuntarily.

"This is my eldest daughter," John introduced. "Heidi. My other is away at Whitman." And oh how he loved to tell people. It was the second time he'd squeezed it into his very brief conversations with Thea now. "Heidi, these are our new neighbors. Thea and — Bree, was it?"

Bryce smiled amicably, but Thea knew her well enough to spot the irritation sparkling in those brown eyes, made golden in the midday sunlight. "Bryce."

"Bryce. That's right." John placed Sugarplum down at his feet, and she scurried off to chase a butterfly hovering around a cluster of sweet peas curling up the trellis. "Thea's mother owns the bookstore on Fothergill Street."

"I haven't had a chance to visit yet," Heidi replied. She shook Thea's hand, her fingers soft and nails painted seafoam blue. Thea could scent floral perfume wafting off her, as powdery and sweet as the rain-watered hydrangeas. "Good to meet you both. Are you staying for the barbecue?"

"Oh, we only came to —" Bryce began, but Thea cut her off.

"If you'll have us! I'm starved." A lie. Thea and Bryce had sliced off a chunk of lasagna before bringing it here, and snuck a few brownies in on the way for dessert. Still, she *had* come here to investigate, and how could she, if she didn't stay for a hotdog or two?

Bryce's narrowed eyes burned into her, and Thea tried to ignore them, face feeling slightly hotter than it had a moment ago under both women's stares.

"Of course! Excuse me while I get everything ready. I'll

warm up the lasagna, too!" John strolled away with Sugarplum following at his loafers, disappearing back into the house. It was a newly renovated house, something Thea had seen scaffolding around for years, now, and it showed in the large windows and tidy brickwork. Most of the other homes in town were old and crooked or else on their way to being demolished completely.

"So what is it you do, Thea?" Heidi pushed her sunglasses onto her head. Free from the shades, her eyes were an electrifying blue that seemed to hold Thea in their icy grip.

"Oh, I work at the bookstore with my mom," she replied, working hard to steady her voice. "And I present a podcast, too."

Bryce cleared her throat. "*We* present a podcast."

"That sounds interesting!" Heidi's focus didn't stray from Thea, and Thea could feel Bryce bristle beside her. "What's it about?"

"True crime," said Thea.

"*Murder*," said Bryce, in a cold warning tone that she usually only used when Thea had woken her up before seven.

"What about..." Thea continued, as she glanced bewilderedly at her best friend, then "...you?" back at Heidi. Bryce's jaw had been clenched as she scowled at their new neighbor, her arms crossed over her chest. Thea frowned, clueless as to what had sparked Bryce's sudden hostility.

Heidi seemed to be oblivious to the tension. "Oh, I used to work in a boutique," she said cheerfully, "but there aren't many fashion opportunities here so I just got a job at that cocktail bar around the corner. The Bloody Mary?"

Thea's stomach flipped with excitement. "*We're* headed there tomorrow night!"

"Great. I guess I'll see you there." Heidi scanned Thea from head to toe. She must've liked whatever she saw, because she smiled before drawing away. "I better go help out Dad. I'll be back."

Thea could only nod and watch her swaying hips as she wandered back to the house.

Beside her, Bryce scoffed and examined her chipped fingernails sourly. "Jesus. Want me to leave you two alone?"

"What?" Thea blinked away the Heidi-induced haze, snapping her gaze back to her best friend.

"I thought we came here to deliver lasagna and snoop, not flirt with the daughter of the guy you thought was a murderer not five minutes ago."

"I wasn't flirting," Thea protested, though it came out mangled and unconvincing.

"Uh-huh," hummed Bryce with a roll of her eyes. "I have better things to do with my day than this, so —"

"*Look,*" gasped Thea, pinching Bryce's wrist as she gestured to a small, ramshackle shed in the very corner of the yard. Shadows from the overhanging willows covered most of it, and what didn't was infested by ivy and weeds. "Don't tell me that you wouldn't hide body parts there."

"I can say with absolute certainty that I have never hidden body parts anywhere, nor do I plan to. Besides," Bryce sighed, "if he was using that shed, the plants would be disturbed."

"Okay, Sherlock. Maybe he just wants you to think that."

Silvery cobwebs winked at Thea in the dappled light, as though they knew something she didn't. She glanced back over her shoulder to make sure John and Heidi were still inside before inching towards the shed and clearing the curling ivy out of the fogged window to peer inside. All she saw were shadows and a few rusted gardening tools that must've been left by the previous owner.

Ugh. Thea hated it when Bryce was right.

"Thea," called Bryce, but Thea ignored her to round the shed. The soil was more damp here, the stench mossy and a little too much like wild animal urine for her tastes. There were no disturbed patches of grass, though, and not even the dandelions had been trampled on by anyone — but her, now.

"Okay." She accepted defeat, trudging her way back around the shed and trying not to clothesline herself on the clawing tree branches in the process. "Maybe not such serial killer vibes after all. Maybe they have, like, an attic or something where they keep people's head — oh!"

Thea came to an abrupt standstill, heart racing until she had to press her hand to her chest to steady it. A middle-aged, dark-haired man waited for her by the door of the shed wearing an amused, lopsided grin. "I assure you there are no heads in our shed *or* our attic. There are no body parts at all, for that matter — and if there are, it'll be time to sue the estate agent who sold us the place."

"Oh, good!" John exclaimed, lemonade brimming across the rim of a large pitcher as he made his way back into the yard. "You've met our guests. This is my husband, Aiden."

Husband? So not only had Thea made a fool of herself and accused the new neighbors of hiding body parts, but her usually perfectly functioning gaydar was faulty. Behind Aiden, Bryce's cheeks were swollen with a trapped peal of laughter.

Face flaming, Thea pasted a sheepish smile on her face and wiggled her fingers. "Hi. I'm Thea. I was just, er, checking for termites. I thought I heard one down here."

"Yes, Thea freelances in termite extermination," Bryce said. "She's pest *obsessed,* actually, and has very sharp hearing."

"Oh, I see," nodded Aiden, biting down on his lower lip as he aided Thea out of the bramble and back onto the grass. "I thought you were just looking for some fresh corpses."

"No." Thea shook her head as though the idea was absolutely ridiculous, working hard not to meet John's puzzled gaze. "Nope, I was just... y'know, looking for termites, but it looks like you're all good here."

"Well that's a relief," John said, setting down plates on the patio table.

Thea returned to Bryce and elbowed her forcefully in her ample stomach. "You know, I don't think we can stay for dinner after all. I just remembered I'm covering my mom's shift at the bookstore later. Enjoy the lasagna, though!"

"Oh," frowned John, watching as Thea dragged Bryce out of the garden. Her face was still burning hot, palms sweaty, and Bryce was hissing out suppressed laughs that only made Thea feel worse.

"I hate you," she said through gritted teeth, as they marched down the street and away from the Godfrey residence.

"Just be glad your new crush wasn't there to witness it."

Though Thea refused to acknowledge talk of a 'crush' — as though they were twelve again and giggling over the school sports teams — she *was* glad that Heidi hadn't been there to witness it. "I don't know what you're talking about."

"*Sure.* Still think they killed Isaac? Because they don't really seem like the 'dump a body in the sewers' type to me, is all."

Thea ground her molars together, and without turning back, replied, "I'm not ruling any suspects out yet."

Bryce only let out another strained chuckle — and the sound followed Thea all the way back to the bookstore.

THREE

When Bryce sat down at her sister's laptop for the first time in months, she had hundreds of emails waiting for her. She'd really only opened the thing in the first place to see what people were saying about Isaac's death, whether there would be a town funeral she could attend, whether there were any leads yet — *and* had found her screensaver had been changed from the standard slideshow of landscapes and sunsets to a photograph of Harry Styles on the cover of *Vogue*.

Teenagers.

There hadn't been much to see, so now she sat methodically deleting each email, most of them discount codes for clothing sites she might've bought something from once and never bothered with again. The PDF version of a community college prospectus sat there, too, untouched since she'd signed herself up onto the mailing list after graduation. There would never be enough time in a day to go back to school now, and even if she did, she had no idea what she'd study. Media, maybe. Film.

And then what? the stiff, pragmatic voice in her head that always kept her from dreaming too big snapped back at the thought. *How are you going to pay for Liv's college with only a diploma in watching things?*

The answer was, she wouldn't. Stone Grange wasn't known for its successful, well-paid artists. It was known for hard workers, laborers, people just trying to scrape by in any minimum wage job they could find. That was all Bryce would ever have. It was better not to even hope, better not to dream. *This* was her life. There was no changing it now.

An unfamiliar email snagged her interest away from her

depressing reality for a moment. Somebody named Genevieve Cox, with the subject line: '**Potential Job Opportunity from an Avid Fan of *Perfect Crimes*!**'

Brows furrowing, Bryce clicked open the email, noticing the avatar beside the name was the well-known, blood spattered logo of Horror Town Studios. Bryce listened to some of their popular podcasts and watched the odd YouTube video reporting unsolved mysteries, but it was Thea who raved about their graphic novels and short films. Though Bryce didn't know why, her heart began to race.

'*Miss Nicholls,*' read the email. '*I hope this finds you well. I am writing with an exciting job opportunity I thought you would be interested in. Horror Town Studios Ltd. are hoping to begin production on a new docuseries exploring some of the most horrific and intriguing crimes and mysteries around the United States. After listening to your podcast,* Perfect Crimes *(great name, by the way), I think you would prove a valuable asset and interesting presenter for the show. I hope it wasn't too forward of me to contact you via email, but it was the only personal up-to-date information I could find on the podcast's social media pages. I'm aware that you work with your co-presenter, Thea Curtis, but please note that this offer extends only to you. If you're interested or have any questions, please contact me at your earliest convenience.*

Regards, Genevieve.'

The color drained from Bryce's face at the mention of Thea. *The offer extends only to you.*

Before she could even analyze what that meant, reason began to kick in; gloomy, cynical clouds dampening any bit of hope Bryce had. It *had* to be some sort of scam. There was no way someone who worked for one of the most widely-known horror providers in the country would *listen* to Bryce and Thea's podcast, much less like it enough to offer Bryce (and *only* Bryce) a job.

She sipped her coffee, letting the cheap, bitter, barely dissolved granules bring her back down to earth. No. No way was this email meant for her.

Even so, her fingers itched at the keyboard. She opened

a new tab without thinking, typing Genevieve's name into the search engine. A portrait of a red-haired woman wearing a pin-stripe suit popped up, next to it, the exact same Horror Town logo as her avatar. All of the details — email, phone number, address — that had been pinned to the bottom of her email were the same here, too.

If it was a scam, it was a damn good one.

"Who's that?"

Bryce slammed the laptop shut when Liv sauntered into the kitchen, shucking off her backpack and jacket. Bryce hadn't even heard her come in, though she was so used to the regular, three o' clock opening of the front door that it probably no longer registered.

"No one," she said, turning her attention to her sister. "How was school?"

"Don't tell me your latest celebrity crush is some badly dressed CEO." Liv sat at the kitchen table and pulled the laptop toward her.

Bryce knew better than to even bother trying to stop her, though her features hardened to a glare. "Snoop. A CEO is better than a boy-band member, anyway."

"If you were at all cultured, you'd know One Direction split up in 2016. Tragic as it is, he isn't a boy-band member anymore." Liv's dark eyes narrowed, face awash in the silvery light of the screen. "Who's Genevieve Cox?"

"Some producer. Hey, how do you know if an email is sham mail or whatever you call it?"

Liv snorted. "Spam?"

"Yeah, that." Bryce waved a dismissive hand and poured her tepid coffee into the sink.

"You mean this email?"

Bryce peered over her sister's shoulder as she switched tabs, back to the email that had sparked all this in the first place.

"This is from, like, three months ago," Liv pointed out as she scanned over the message. "Don't you read your emails?"

"No," admitted Bryce, tucking her lip beneath her teeth anxiously. She hated how badly she wanted Liv to tell her it looked real. How badly she wanted it to *be* real.

"Well, it seems legit. All the details are the same and they're not asking you to click any sus links. Hey, you're going to be famous before me."

Bryce snorted at that, straightening when her back began to ache. "Yeah, right."

"Have you told Thea?" Liv turned away from the laptop and kicked her legs up onto the chair beside her.

"No. I only *just* saw it. Besides, there must be some kind of mistake. Why would they want *me*?"

With a shrug, Liv flicked her braided hair off her shoulders. "Maybe you should ask."

Bryce eyed the email, gulping down the jitters rising in her throat before they could swallow her whole. She supposed there was no harm in asking. Clarifying. It wasn't as though she would accept it either way, not without Thea, but knowing whether she actually had a chance...

God, she was being ridiculous. These things didn't happen to her, and she was letting herself want something that hadn't been made for her. A bad idea. She wouldn't keep entertaining it.

To be sure of it, she closed the laptop a final time. "Hey, what are you doing tonight?"

Liv groaned like the attitude-filled teenager she was. "I'm not hanging out with you, if that's what you think. I have a social life, you know."

"Good. So do I."

"Watching *Scream* with the curtains drawn so you can crush on Neve Campbell does not count as a social life."

Bryce gave her sister a playful slap on the back of her head at that, though she couldn't blame her for assuming those were her only plans, since they would've been, on any other weekend. "I'm going for a few drinks with Thea and Mikey and I don't know what time I'll be home. I'll try not to make it late."

Liv's eyes brightened, a fact that only made Bryce regret her agreement to go even more. "Make it as late as you like. You're allowed to have fun, y'know. You're turning into an old woman."

"Yeah, well, it's *you* who's aging me." It wasn't exactly a lie, either. Bryce didn't *feel* twenty-six — not at home, anyway. It was easier to pretend she was still young with Thea around, but she would always come home to these responsibilities. And she didn't blame her sister for them, but she *was* the reason why. Bryce had been turned into a mother before she'd ever gotten a real chance to be a sister, and after sixteen years, it was … tiring. "And whatever *you* have planned, by the way, the answer is no."

Liv scowled. "I was only going to ask if I could invite a few friends round so I wouldn't be alone in the house all night."

Bryce deliberated this with a huff of displeasure. "How many friends?"

"Four."

"Two."

"Three."

Bryce's shoulders sagged in resignation, and she had to remind herself that it was good Liv had at least asked her. Most teenagers wouldn't. "Can I trust you?"

"You know you can."

With those pleading brown eyes, it was impossible for Bryce to imagine Liv getting up to no good. Not without telling her. They'd always been honest with one another. Bryce had rarely scolded her for anything other than being a general pain in the ass, but then, all kids were a pain in the ass.

"Fine. No drink —"

"No drinking," Liv rattled off before Bryce could spit out the rules, "no drugs, no sex. I know."

"You bet your ass no sex!" Bryce guffawed at the mere mention. "What are you doing, amending my rules? Who ever mentioned sex? You know what, don't answer that." She waved her hands in disgust. "Just don't go out after dark. It's not safe right now."

"I won't. I'll be in my PJs by nine, drinking strictly soda and watching a Disney movie." With a grin, Liv batted her lashes innocently.

"I mean it, Liv." Bryce jabbed her finger out in front of her, feeling far too much like the old lady across the street who yelled at the kids to get off her lawn. "I'm trusting you. Don't make me regret it."

"Can I at least do your makeup?"

Bryce grimaced at that, realizing only now that going out meant she should probably make at least *some* effort with her appearance. That wasn't something she did often, both for a lack of energy and a lack of time. She didn't even own a dress.

"Fine," she agreed warily. "But no eyeliner."

＊ ＊ ＊

"Oh, God. He's wearing eyeliner," grimaced Thea, as Mikey approached the bar. "This is serious."

"And combat boots," agreed Bryce, motioning to their friend's feet.

Indeed, Mikey had strayed dramatically from his usual colorful graphic tees and Converse low-tops. He'd worn all black tonight; his frayed jeans were tucked into well-worn, scuffed platform boots and his hazel eyes had been ringed with smokey makeup.

"Is he trying to *date* Hannah or *be* her?" Thea downed her shot of tequila before Bryce could answer, and then handed Bryce's over so she could do the same.

The Bloody Mary was about as dark and dingy as it sounded. A depressing Nick Cave song droned from a speaker somewhere, and all of the cocktails were horror themed: their Zombie cocktails had been served in a skull-shaped mug, something questionable and eyeball-like floating around inside. It was like being at an off-season Halloween party, with fake cobwebs — Thea hoped they were fake, anyway — catching in their hair and the staff costumed in bloodied rags and skeletal facepaint.

Thea's and Bryce's paradise, really. Mikey would've fit right in if he didn't look so completely un-Mikey in his new get-up.

"Mikey!" Thea greeted when he finally reached them — and soon regretted opening her mouth at all. A pungent whiff of too much cologne choked her half to death. "Jesus. Have you been rolling around in potpourri?"

"Too much?" Mikey winced and adjusted the hem of his Rolling Stones T-shirt, flashing a set of thick, silver rings on his fingers. "I was kind of hoping that if I wore enough cologne, she'd smell me before she saw me, y'know?"

"That makes no sense." Bryce's features, done up in warm brown shadows and glittery highlights for tonight by Olivia, crumpled into a frown. Thea had been taken aback when Bryce got into the cab they'd shared on the way here. It had been a long time since she'd last seen her made up, and with deep red lipstick and her wavy hair freed of its usual loose ponytail, it only reminded Thea of just how beautiful her best friend was.

And just how much Thea's stomach could lurch at the mere sight of her.

"You know what?" Mikey huffed, scraping his shoulder-length hair from his eyes. He'd left it down tonight, too, though it wasn't quite as majestic as Bryce's. "So far, the two of you are crappy wingwomen. Have you seen her yet?"

"I can barely see my own hand with the fog machine on over there." Bryce motioned to the corner, where puffs of smoke spurted onto the tiny dancefloor. Thea couldn't help but notice that she hadn't taken so much as a sip of either of her drinks yet. The shot still swished in her hand, the cocktail still brimming on the bar with a straw sinking sadly into the orange liquid. Thea had almost finished hers already.

"I'm going to the bathroom. Order me something fruity, will you?"

Mikey still fidgeted on his way to the men's room, and Thea pitied him. Her own nervous energy manifested through excessive chit-chat and giggling, but poor Mikey couldn't disguise his so easily. It was written all over him.

Turning back to the sticky, crowded bar, Thea ordered another round of drinks from a tall man wearing Beetlejuice-style pinstripes. He looked vaguely familiar, but with the facepaint, she couldn't place why. A new acquaintance, or an old school friend, maybe. She wouldn't have been the first to remain trapped in this bleak little town.

Bryce was oblivious, too busy scanning the bustling crowd of people piling in with a sour glare.

"Can't you at least pretend you're having fun?" Thea sighed.

Bryce's dark eyes snapped to her, and she moved to place the tequila back on her beermat.

"No!" Thea stopped her, her clammy fingers curling around Bryce's wrist and directing the drink back towards her lips. "The drinks cost a fortune here. You're not wasting my hard-earned money."

"Then *you* have it," scowled Bryce, still trying to struggle against Thea's grip. The tequila spilled over the rim of the shot glass and splashed onto Bryce's hand and dribbled down her bare arm, until they both shied away from further spillages.

Bryce wore a plain black camisole top under a collarless T-shirt and skinny jeans, and yet with the soft curves of her hips and thighs, she still managed to be one of the most beautiful women in the Bloody Mary. Thea herself had opted for color and shimmer, in a loose champagne-hued party dress she'd been dying for a chance to wear since she'd bought it on sale last Christmas. Perhaps it was a little fancy for a rundown bar in Stone Grange, but it was better than her usual faded jeans.

"No," Thea whined. "Come on, Bryce. You can't let loose for one night?"

"What if Liv calls?" Bryce sucked the tequila from her fingers, leaving a lipstick stain across her knuckle in the process. "What if she needs me? I can't go home wasted."

"*Bryce.*" Thea rested her hands on Bryce's shoulders, blinking up at her with a deadpan expression. "She's sixteen. She's with her friends. She'll probably make better life choices tonight than I will. Have a night off. You've earned it."

With a huff, Bryce nodded and brought the shot to her lips. She swallowed it down in one, wincing against the burn. "This is peer pressure."

Thea cheered her support. "That's my girl."

The next round of drinks had arrived by then and the sugary smell of Bryce's floral perfume wafted over Thea without warning as she tossed back her hair to take her second shot. Thea faltered, wrapped in it, in *her,* and as Bryce laughed suddenly, Thea wondered how long it had been since Bryce had truly felt free of the weight of her responsibilities. It had certainly been a while since she'd seen her best friend *appear* this relaxed, which, to Thea's standard, was not very relaxed at all, mind you. Now tequila trickled down Bryce's chin, and Thea caught it with the pad of her thumb before it could go any further.

Bryce froze beneath her touch, eyes fluttering half-closed to eye Thea's pink-polished thumbnail. Resting in the small dimple of her chin, it was close enough to her scarlet-stained lips that Thea could feel Bryce's breath tickling her.

"Sorry." Thea drew away and hoped that her glowing cheeks weren't too obvious in the dim light.

If they were, Bryce gave no sign, but the corner of her mouth softened with a grin. "Thanks."

Thea nodded, eyes lingering on her best friend for perhaps a little too long, but she couldn't tear away from this version of her. A version she rarely got to see.

"What?" Bryce's brows knitted together.

"Just…" Thea shook her head to free herself from her Bryce-induced daze. "Nothing. I just like it when you let your hair down. Literally and figuratively."

Bryce's lips parted as though to reply, but something beyond Thea snagged her attention away. She pointed with little subtlety to the same direction Mikey had just disappeared to. "Isn't that Mikey's girl?"

Turning, Thea scoured the sea of bobbing heads, having to rise to her tiptoes to get a good look. But yes, there she was, a striking, dark-haired woman with smokey eyes and a ruffled black shirt sipped on a murky espresso martini and chatted with a group of friends. "That's her. Come on."

She grabbed Bryce by the hand and weaved through the bar, bones rattling in time to the tune of 'Monster Mash', which boomed louder in this corner of the room. Thea was so focused on not losing sight of Hannah that she toppled headfirst into another tall, disgustingly damp human frame.

"Oof!" Bryce puffed behind her as she knocked into Thea. And then: "Did you fall *down* the toilet, Mikey?"

When Thea adjusted to the mottled gray haze of the fog machine, she realized that the person she'd bumped into was, thankfully, Mikey, and he *did* look as though he'd taken a detour somewhere wet. The neckline of his shirt was ringed with a darker splotch, and two identical patches bled beneath his armpits.

"You made me all paranoid so I tried to wash off my cologne."

"You..." There were simply no words Thea could find in response. She glanced down and found a crumpled sheet of tissue stuck to his boot. "There's toilet paper on your shoe. Come here."

She stepped on the tissue with the toe of her white Converse, and Mikey swore as he freed himself from the soggy, unwelcome hanger-on. "Jesus. Why am I like this? What was I thinking? I can't talk to her."

"You're a twenty-five-year-old man, Mikey," said Bryce, brushing past Thea to reach him. "I'm absolutely certain you can talk to other humans. You talk to *us* all the time."

"Right." His throat bobbed as he swallowed. "And you're way scarier."

"Hey!" argued Thea. "*She* is. *I'm* not. Anyway, she's right there." She attempted to gesture casually to Hannah's table, where a raucous amount of laughter echoed over the music.

"Oh, no." Mikey clawed at his collar, a sheen of sweat beginning to stick to his forehead. "This was a mistake. I can't just go up there and talk to her. You're brave, Bryce. You do it for me."

"If *I* do it for you, *I'll* be the one taking her on a date," Bryce deadpanned, and Thea couldn't help but cast her a troubled scowl. "What?! She's hot!"

Hannah *was* hot in an intimidating, witchy, Nineties, *The*

Craft sort of way, but she was hoping Bryce hadn't noticed that, or at least hoped she wouldn't say so in front of Thea for the sake of Thea's self-esteem.

Thea rolled her eyes and linked her arm through Mikey's. "All right. Time to fulfill my wingwoman duties."

"Wait, what?" Mikey tried to wriggle out of her grasp, but Thea's grip remained tight as iron shackles. She refused to let him bow out now. She pulled him towards the group with a wide, friendly grin, slotting herself in between a woman in the middle of taming her curly bangs and a man with a buzzcut at the table.

"Hey, guys. This is our first time here and the drinks look a little," she shuddered, "icky. Any recommendations?"

"Oh, you should totally try the Franken-lime," a red-haired woman beside Hannah suggested. Hannah looked too interested in mixing her own murky drink to notice their presence at all, and Thea narrowed her eyes determinedly. She stepped on Mikey's foot to urge him to speak, and Mikey cried out a mangled show of surprise-turned-pain.

"Ow!"

Hopeless. He was hopeless. Thea searched for Bryce's assistance, but her best friend was nowhere in sight, and another exclamation from the table distracted her from looking more thoroughly.

"Hey!" It came from the broad man with the blond buzzcut beside her. He was looking up at her, the corner of his eyebrow puckered with a silver stud. "Aren't you that podcaster?"

Everyone's attention fell to them then, including Hannah's, though with her chin in her palm, she still seemed bored.

"Yeah, you are!" the guy continued. "You host *Perfect Crimes!*"

The fact that anyone recognized Thea and her podcast stunned her into silence for a moment. He must've followed their social media to know what she looked like at all, or else be skilled at identifying someone just by their voice. "You listen to us?"

"Every week. Oh, man, I love that show. I was telling you guys about it, remember?"

They all nodded, exploding into muffled whispers of excitement.

"Well…" Thea's gaze shifted back to Hannah, who had perked up slightly. She patted Mikey on the back, thrusting him forward in the process. "*This* guy does all the important stuff for us. He's our producer."

"It's good to meet you, dude. I'm Jace." The man extended his hand, and Mikey shook it timidly, a splodge of pink blossoming across either cheek. "Come sit with us. Have a drink."

My work here is done. Thea slowly inched away as they began questioning Mikey about the podcast. If Hannah wasn't interested, he at least had a pretty good chance with *someone* at the table.

A proud wingwoman, Thea clapped her hands together as though finishing up a hard day's work and began her search for Bryce again. It was cut short when she stumbled into one of the waitresses holding a tray of crimson cocktails.

"Oh!" Thea lifted her hands to steady herself, but it was too late. She'd walked right into the tray of drinks, and the person holding them. The glasses clattered and sploshed across Thea's dress, leaving stains of red across the shimmery fabric. To top it off, she was decorated with celery sticks.

"Oh, no!" Two hands patted her down with a napkin, the tray and shattered glasses left abandoned in a puddle on the floor. "I'm sorry. I'm so sorry. It's my first shift and —"

But Thea wasn't listening to the slur of panicked apologies. She recognized the ashy blonde hair and the pink cupid's bow lips. Recognized the light eyes rising to meet her own.

"Heidi?"

Heidi frowned, and then recognition dawned across her features. "Thea!"

She wasn't dressed up like the others, though she'd clearly tried to fit in, with a trickle of red lipstick zigzagging down the corner of her mouth.

"Hey!" A surprise laugh bubbled from Thea as she wiped her dress down. It made no difference, except in smudging the stain more. The dress was well and truly ruined.

"Oh, no." Heidi nibbled her bottom lip as she eyed the mess, swiping celery from her shoulder. "Your dress. I'm so, so sorry. I'm no good at this waitressing thing."

"No harm done. Here, let me help you." They crouched together and nearly knocked heads in the process, glasses clinking as they scrambled carefully to pick them up.

"Is your friend here, too?"

"Somewhere." Thea craned her neck to search for Bryce again, but found her nowhere to be seen. "Knowing her, she probably snuck into a cab and is already at home in her pajamas."

"Not a party person?"

"Nah. We prefer murder."

Heidi's eyes widened in alarm, and Thea's cheeks burned as she sputtered out a correction.

"I mean horror movies and true crime podcasts, not *actual* homicide."

"Oh." Heidi chuckled in relief and began weaving her way to the bar. Thea followed her, feeling out of place suddenly. Her dress clung to her stomach, the damp material chafing against her skin. Any sane person would have already been headed for the nearest hand dryer, but clearly Thea was an idiot who didn't know when a conversation was over.

"Enjoying your first shift?"

Heidi blew a strand of hair from her face. "It's... challenging. I'm already kinda sick of hearing the same three Michael Jackson songs on repeat."

"Thriller" was currently blaring now, and a group of drunk, rowdy friends had taken to the tiny dance floor to show off their best approximation of the famous choreography beneath the strobe lights. "Also, I think the fog machine is setting off my allergies."

"I can keep you company for a while..." Thea suggested with a wry smile. "If you'd like."

Heidi's eyes glittered. "I'd like that," she said.

* * *

Bryce had only been here an hour, and she was already tired; mostly because of her co-worker Peter. He'd spotted her and pulled her aside when Thea was guiding Mikey to Hannah's table, and she'd lost them both when he insisted on buying her a drink. He hadn't stopped talking since. Now, she was three Franken-limes down and cotton balls swathed her brain, not made any better by the booming music and rowdy, drunk crowd.

She rested her head in her hand, elbow digging into the bar as Peter swirled his finger around the rim of his glass.

"I'm so glad I bumped into you tonight," he said. "I had no idea you could be this much fun."

Bryce tried not to take offense to that, sipping her drink from the straw pressed between her lips. She checked her phone for the umpteenth time that night and found no missed calls or texts. According to the update she'd received from Liv half an hour ago, she and her three friends were watching a movie at home, completely fine. She knew she should stop worrying, that Liv was growing up and Bryce could trust her for one night, but anxiety still roared in her chest at the thought of her alone with her friends, getting up to whatever awful things teenagers got up to.

At Liv's age, Bryce certainly hadn't been watching movies on a Friday night, anyway.

"Yeah."

"Are you working tomorrow?"

"Yep," she sighed. Luckily, her shift didn't start until noon, so she wouldn't have to wake too early. A good thing if Peter was going to keep buying her drinks.

"You know, we never really talked about that date I asked you on." Peter's coarse hand fell to her knee, and she eyed the touch warily. "No Thai food, right?"

"You know, Peter, I don't really have time to date." She looped her fingers around his wrist and removed his hand before it wandered somewhere else. "I think we should just be friends."

"Oh." He blinked; cleared his throat; scratched the back of his neck. "Right. Sure."

Bryce almost apologized, but then decided against it. What did she have to be sorry for? She had never led Peter on or done anything to make him assume they could be an item. She was being honest. She didn't owe him any more than that.

"So do you maybe want to hang out another time... as friends?" he continued.

"Maybe." Noncommittal, she just shrugged, then checked her phone again. Still nothing. Though she knew Liv would probably be telling her friends how clingy and annoying her big sister was, she began to type out another message. Her fingers were clumsy, and it ended up as a distorted version of "**Are you okay?**" riddled with typos and random emojis.

Pressure began to build on her bladder, a result of too many cocktails downed too quickly, and she groaned as she slid off the barstool.

"I'm going to head to the bathroom," she shouted above the music, which had transitioned from Halloween party to dance and electronica. "I'll see you later, Peter."

"Well, let me help you." Peter rose with her and placed his hands at the small of her back as she stumbled her way through the crowd.

"I don't think you're allowed in the ladies' room." She paused when a familiar head of straightened red-gold hair caught her attention. Thea was leaning across the edge of the bar, laughing, with a pretty bartender who Bryce had only met once. Heidi.

Her usual filter corroded by the alcohol, Bryce scoffed out her disgust. She didn't quite know what she was disgusted at, only that each time Thea turned into a gooey, starry-eyed mess in front of a pretty woman, it left something achingly heavy in her gut. Second-hand embarrassment, maybe.

Definitely not jealousy, anyway.

"You okay?" Peter raised a brow, still bracing his hands on her hips to steady her, though she wasn't *that* drunk. Just dizzy.

Just swaying. Just a little bit nauseous and a little bit regretful over that third Franken-lime.

"Uh-huh," nodded Bryce, pushing Peter's hands away and brushing past Thea without a word. "Peachy. See you later, Peter."

She walked quickly into the disinfectant-laced hallway, the pulse of the music ebbing when the door fell shut. Peter was left on the other side, and she hoped it stayed that way. She pushed through to the ladies' room before he could follow.

Someone was washing their hands at the sinks, and Bryce struggled to recognize her through her alcohol-induced haze.

"Hey," she finally muttered, leaning lazily against the wall. "You're Mikey's Hannah."

Hannah frowned, eyes lifting in the mirror to meet Bryce's as she shook the excess water from her hands. "Who?"

"Mikey. My friend."

"You mean that guy with the," her finger traced a halo around the crown of her head, "hair?"

"Yeah. He wore combat boots for you." With that, Bryce sauntered into the stall, checking her phone as she relieved herself. No texts. Panic began to build in her, fueled slightly by the booze. When she was done, she wandered back out into an empty bathroom to wash her hands and then dialled her sister's number.

It rang. No answer.

Bryce texted her again.

'**Ppck up thw pkone pls!!!**' she wrote in a haphazard clicking of letters, and then added a few thumbs up emojis for good measure.

Ugh. Bryce's stomach was churning, and not just from the Franken-limes. Her sister was home alone, Thea had abandoned her for a prettier, nicer woman, and she was too drunk. *And* Peter was probably still waiting for her at the door.

She whirled around as the door was thrown open, the handle denting the plaster of the wall from the force.

"Peter's waiting for you outside the door." Thea entered scowling, her dress stained red. Her cheeks were much the same shade, too.

"What happened to *you?*"

Thea switched on the faucet, swishing water across her torso with a huff. "I bumped into Heidi when she was carrying a tray of Bloody Marys."

"Ah, yes, Heidi," hummed Bryce, sourness lacing her tone. *"That's* why you disappeared."

"It was *you* who disappeared, actually." Thea began dabbing at her dress with tissue, but it did absolutely nothing but leave lint peppering her dress. Bryce sighed and pulled a mile's worth of paper towels from the dispenser, dampening it with soap before trying to help. "With *Peter.*"

"I did no such thing."

The dress was a lost cause, so Bryce abandoned the paper towels in the sink. The stain had only faded slightly, and there was no way her clumsy hands could get it out with only cheap hand wash. Besides, a celery stick was still snagged on the gauzy fabric of the skirt and Bryce had skipped dinner, so she plucked it free and bit on the crunchy end without thinking.

"You're drunk," Thea observed.

"You're drunk. And you're in love with Heidi. Why is there celery in your dress?"

Thea wrinkled her nose, and it only reminded Bryce of how much she missed her usual freckles when they were covered by makeup. "No. *You're* in love with *Peter.* And I already told you. Bloody Marys."

"I came in here to *escape* Peter." The stale celery wasn't helping Bryce's unsettled stomach. She threw the remains into the trash can and pulled out her phone again. Still no new text messages. It was only midnight, so she doubted Liv would already be asleep. She could think of no other reason why she wouldn't be answering her drunk, concerned, sister's texts. "And to call Liv. She isn't picking up."

"I bet she's just busy with her friends."

"I shouldn't have left her alone." Her hands shook as she dialled Liv's number again. It went straight to voicemail this time, and her heart plummeted. "Her phone's turned off. I have to go.

Something might've —"

"Bryce." Thea's warm, damp hands curled around her own, gently, tying Bryce's frayed nerves back together until she could breathe again. "She's okay."

"I have to go home." Tears pricked Bryce's eyes. Because she couldn't have just one night off. Because she couldn't just relax and be the fun best friend Thea wanted her to be. Because she had to be sensible and serious and a mother when she hadn't even had anyone to teach her how to do it properly.

"Then let's go home." One of Thea's hands tangled with Bryce's while the other combed soothingly through her hair. "It's okay. Let's go home."

Bryce nodded and let Thea guide her wobbly frame back through the bar. She hid herself from Peter, who now sat on a barstool talking to the naggingly-familiar-but-she-still-couldn't-place-him bartender dressed as Beetlejuice, and sent a quick wave to Mikey, who was too invested in a conversation with Hannah's friends to notice. And then they fell out into the cold night, and Bryce let Thea hold her up then, too. All the way home.

❈ ❈ ❈

Apparently, Thea had given Liv too much credit in telling Bryce she'd be okay on her own. A trashed house awaited them when they got back to Bryce's, empty beer bottles collecting on the floor and crushed bags of chips spilling out onto the patchwork settee. A few kids Thea had never seen before were passed out on top of the mess, a rerun of some trashy reality show blaring from the TV. She found the remote wedged between the arm of a teenage girl who snored loudly and turned it off. None of them stirred.

She felt Bryce suck in a sharp breath behind her, straightening as though the sight was enough to sober her up immediately.

"You've got to be kidding me." Bryce toed one of the beer bottles, glassy eyes blazing with anger. "I'm going to kill her."

"Bryce —" Thea began, but it was too late. Bryce marched

through the living room and down the corridor in as straight a line as she could manage and flung open the door to Liv's bedroom. Thea half-expected smoke to curl from her ears with all the anger that bristled from her.

"Olivia Grace Nicholls, get your ass out of bed *now!*" Bryce flicked on the light, the room spilling with an intensely bright wash of yellow.

Liv poked her dishevelled head out from beneath her covers, revealing a friend on either side of her who appeared equally as confused. She yawned without bothering to cover her mouth. "What?"

"'What?'" Bryce repeated, voice rising to a piercing crescendo. "'*What?*'"

"Bryce." Liv pushed the covers back, revealing her pajama shorts. The other girls were still dressed and wide-eyed. Good. They should be afraid of Bryce. In this state, Thea sure as hell was. "Calm down."

Thea reached to touch Bryce's arm, but Bryce snatched it away.

"No, Liv, I won't *calm down!*" So much rage trembled in Bryce's voice that Thea began to wonder if she should start hiding any sharp or heavy objects. "I trusted you for *one* night, and you betrayed me."

"You *said* I could have friends over," frowned Liv.

"And either I can't count, or there's a hell of a lot more than the three people we agreed upon in here. And I said *no drinking!*"

Liv's face drained of color, eyes darting to her friends and then back again. Clearly, she hadn't expected to have been caught. In that case, Thea thought, it was a rookie move to have left the empty bottles lying around. The teens were surely smarter than that.

"Bryce," Thea whispered, eyeing Liv's petrified friends with a wince. "Let's talk about this rationally."

"We're *past* rational."

"I didn't *drink* anything." Liv protested, biting down on her trembling lower lip. She would know what this meant to Bryce; it wasn't just about her being underage, but about their mother and all the ways they'd watched her be reckless with drink and drugs. After her own troubled adolescence with much the same problem, Thea knew that Bryce's greatest fear was Liv turning out the same way.

And Liv had done the one thing that would upset Bryce, *break* her, more than anything else.

"And I'm supposed to believe that?" Bryce questioned, upper lip curling in disgust.

"*Yes!*" Liv's voice strained as though she was on the brink of tears.

"It's true, Bryce," said the blonde-haired girl still cowering in Liv's double bed. "*We* all had some, but Liv wouldn't."

"Who bought them?"

They all glanced at one another then as if cursing themselves for not getting their story straight beforehand.

"Who. Bought. Them?" Bryce repeated, voice low and deadly as she glared at each of them in turn.

"Finn brought them." Liv scraped a hand across her tired face, resigned to her grim fate. "He said he'd snuck them out of his dad's fridge."

"Who the fuck is Finn?"

"Just a friend. He came by for a little while."

"Did he?" Bryce cocked her head, jaw clenching. "And how many other *friends* came around tonight to trash my living room?"

Thea had no idea what to do, how to make this better. She could only stand, helpless, while Liv submitted to the onslaught.

"We were *going* to clean it up," Liv said. "But we... we fell asleep."

"Answer the question."

"Bryce," Thea pleaded again, softly. "Let's talk about this properly. She won't answer if you're barking at her."

She regretted her words immediately. Bryce whirled around, and the daggers that had been flying toward Liv now embedded themselves in Thea's flesh. "This has *nothing* to do with you."

"I just think —"

"I don't *care* what you think. You're not a parent."

"Neither are you!" accused Liv, stealing Bryce's attention again. "You're my *sister*."

Bryce recoiled, and Thea with her. "A sister who's raised you when your own parents couldn't be bothered to! And this is what I get for it, is it? Parties and alcohol and a trashed house?"

"You've been drinking, too!"

"I'm twenty-six years old!" Bryce's face turned beetroot red, her scream loud enough to wake the neighbors. "I asked you if I could trust you for *one night,* Olivia! *One night* where I didn't have to worry. *One night* where I could have fun for myself. And you couldn't even let me have that."

Thea heard shuffling behind her, and turned to find the others who had been sleeping on the couch craning their necks to watch the show.

She flashed them a warning look. "Go clean up the living room."

They did, scurrying off as though their lives depended on it.

"Well, maybe *I* wanted that, too," Liv countered, crossing her arms over her chest. "Maybe *I* wanted to be a normal teenager for one night, without my overbearing sister to boss me around."

Bryce pursed her lips, nostrils flaring and fists clenching, and Thea knew the words had cut deeply. All of the effort she made, day in, day out; all of the things she'd sacrificed... she no longer got to be the fun, loving sister any teenage girl would have dreamed of. That privilege had been stripped from her long ago. She had to be a parent, the one who bossed Liv around until she wound up resenting her. Bryce didn't deserve it, and Thea felt the wound as though it was her own.

"Well, I hope you had fun." There was no anger in Bryce's voice now. There was nothing at all, and somehow, that was worse. Her words left an icy draft wafting through the room. "It'll be the only night you get."

Liv rolled her eyes. "Whatever."

"Your friends leave first thing in the morning," Bryce

ordered. "When I get up, I want the house spotless and empty. You're grounded until you learn how to follow my rules. Is that clear?"

Liv only climbed back into bed, her friends shifting uncomfortably beside her. "Turn the light off when you leave."

Bryce scoffed and walked out, Thea following behind. Needless to say, she didn't turn off the light, but she did shut the door with an almighty slam that reverberated through every wall in the house.

One thing was certain: Liv surely wouldn't disobey her sister again any time soon.

* * *

"I think that went reasonably well," Thea said when Bryce shut her own bedroom door and kicked off her boots. Her feet cracked, bone by bone, as they met with the flat, worn carpet, and Bryce let herself shut her eyes against it for a moment.

Her mind hummed and her chest ached and she felt like the worst parent alive. What had she been thinking, trusting a sixteen-year-old at home in an empty house on a Friday night? When Bryce had been sixteen, she'd probably spent more time high and drunk than she had sober.

But Liv was supposed to be different. Bryce believed she'd raised her to be different. Better.

Apparently not.

When she opened her eyes again, she found Thea rooting through Bryce's wardrobe. "Mind if I borrow some PJs?"

"You're staying?"

"Is that okay? I mean... there *is* a potential killer in town."

Bryce had almost forgotten. Somehow, taking care of a teenager seemed far more taxing than dealing with Isaac's murder. "Right. Yeah. No problem."

She could do with the company anyway. She knew from countless late nights together that Thea rambled enough before she fell asleep that it would pull Bryce's attention away from her own seething anger.

"Bryce." Thea's soft voice was unexpected enough that Bryce faltered midway through searching for her makeup remover. Her best friend's blue eyes shone sympathetically, fingers winding around a loose thread from the old, tatty Fleetwood Mac tee in her hands. It would drown Thea, but Thea always seemed to choose Bryce's oldest, most oversized clothes when she stayed over, which was rare these days, anyway.

"Hmm?"

"Don't worry about Liv, okay? She's just being an obnoxious teenager. She knows you only want the best for her."

Bryce gulped down the lump in her throat and finally found her makeup wipes in her bedside drawer. She clawed the heavy eyeshadow and foundation off to distract herself from the churning sadness in her gut. "Yeah. Sorry I had to cut tonight short. And sorry I yelled at you in there."

"I shouldn't have gotten involved."

"No, you were right. I… I lost it. It's just so hard." Her voice cracked traitorously, and she glanced down through stinging tears in the hopes Thea wouldn't notice. "I don't know how to do it right."

"I don't think anyone does, B." Thea skirted through unwashed clothes and work uniforms strewn across the floor to reach Bryce. "You're doing a good job, though. She's lucky to have you."

"It doesn't feel that way."

"I know. I'm sorry." Thea's fingers laced through Bryce's, soft and warm and freckled. And then a kiss was placed on her forehead, stunning Bryce. She lifted her chin, and brushed noses with Thea. It should've been funny and clumsy and silly, but neither of them laughed. She heard Thea's breath catch in her throat, heard her own heart pulsing in her ears. And she couldn't find it in her to just… move away. Let the moment be done with. She needed Thea close to her, needed —

Her eyes fell to Thea's lips, pink and patchy with faded

lipstick. Needed what? She didn't know; only knew that it felt as though lightning bolts were forking through her chest whenever Thea got this close. Because she loved Thea. Because Thea was her friend. Because she needed the comfort, and Thea was always so willing to give it. So she told herself, anyway.

Maybe it's the drink, she thought, as she pulled away and clumsily tried to wipe off her mascara. It was difficult when she was one beat away from bursting into tears. Thea noticed her struggling and took the wipe from her, wiping her eyes gently.

"You're always looking after me," Bryce whispered.

"Someone has to." Thea pulled the wipe away. It was smeared with oranges and blacks and glitter. "You forgot your lipstick."

The cool wet wipe was a soothing surprise against Bryce's cracked lips, and they locked eyes again. Thea's were round and sparkling as mirrorballs, still framed by her own makeup. Her fingers slowed against the wipe, the pad of her thumb following the crease of Bryce's bottom lips. And then pink smattered her cheeks, and Bryce tried to ignore the disappointment she felt when Thea pulled away, throwing the wipe in the wastebasket and turning her back.

Bryce's eyes followed her, though she realized soon enough that they shouldn't have. Thea was shimmying out of her Bloody Mary-stained dress, pulling it up over her arms so that her pale, dainty body was on show. It was nothing that Bryce hadn't seen before, but it still lit a fire in her that she quickly tried to snuff out. She remembered how Thea had looked at her in the bar. The same way she'd looked at her a second ago. Was Bryce reading into it, or was that look too intense for someone who was just supposed to be her best friend?

Her own pajamas were folded in a drawer — a simple gray sweatshirt so old she couldn't remember even buying it anymore. It might have even been her mother's, infested with holes as it was. She undressed quickly, casting Thea a sidelong glance when she peeled off her jeans.

"I hate jeans so much." It was an attempt at breaking the

ice, though it was true enough. The button had left a round dent in the soft flesh below her navel, and the seam had lined the inside of her silver-striped thighs. It might've helped if she could afford a new pair that actually fit her size-fourteen body.

"That's why pajamas exist." Thea, dwarfed in Bryce's old shirt, collapsed onto the bed with a sigh of relief. "Sweet, sweet bliss. Which side are you taking?"

"The wall," Bryce said, pulling her shorts on quickly and tying her hair up. She hated the way it felt when she left it down, like a fleece collar clinging to the back of her neck. "You get up to pee, like, six times during the night."

She turned the main light off and Thea swapped it for the bedside lamp, an old desk one whose bulb was slowly flickering away. Bryce had to climb over Thea to get to her spot, and she did it with little grace, their limbs tangling between the duvet. Comfort washed through her as soon as her head hit the pillow, her eyes fluttering shut so that she could finally escape, if her mind would stop buzzing enough to let her.

Thea turned off the bedside lamp and lay beside her, the smell of her citrus perfume clinging to Bryce's bedsheets in a way Bryce knew she'd still be able to smell tomorrow, when Thea had left and she was alone again.

"I'm sorry you didn't end up having fun tonight," Thea murmured.

Bryce brought her knees to her chest. "I'm sorry my drama ruined it."

"Did anything happen with Peter?"

Bryce frowned. She knew that voice. It was the same voice Thea had used when they'd visited the Godfreys the other day. The voice of someone who was being nosy but trying not to show it. "No. Did anything happen with Heidi?"

"No."

Bryce hated that the answer made her glad. She said nothing, though, instead kicking her legs restlessly. Her body still thrummed with annoyance, made all the worse by the knowledge that there were five other teenagers under her roof tonight who had brought alcohol into the house and trashed the place with their mess.

"Bryce," Thea said, voice a low murmur.

"What?"

She had to stifle a gasp when Thea's hands slipped into hers again, the mattress shifting beneath her as she turned onto her side. She found Thea's eyes gleaming in the moonlight, watching her.

"It's going to be okay. You know that, don't you?"

Bryce didn't know anything anymore, but it was nice just to be told, to be comforted. She so often felt alone in this bed. So she squeezed Thea's hand and let the light circles traced across her arm send her slowly to sleep. She could be angry and worried and exhausted again tomorrow.

Tonight, she would stay wrapped in this blanket of peace with her best friend.

FOUR

"Bryce."

Nausea churned in Thea's gut as she drew her best friend's attention away from washing the dishes. Thea had made scrambled eggs on toast, which had mostly been picked at in a terse silence after Liv's friends had left this morning. She still sat at the kitchen table now, scrolling mindlessly through her phone to put off drying.

There must have been dread trembling in Thea's voice, because Bryce threw the washcloth down and turned from the sud-covered sink with furrowed brows.

"What's wrong?"

Thea cast a sidelong glance towards the living room, where Liv shuffled around, still cleaning up last night's mess. To prevent her from overhearing, Thea lowered her voice. "There was another murder."

Bryce paled and fell into the seat opposite without so much as blinking. "When?"

"Last night. They found the body in a scrapyard just outside of town at six this morning." Thea could've been reading off her *Perfect Crimes* script in the basement — only this was different. This was happening *now,* in their own quiet little town.

"What the hell are you two whispering about now?" Liv called, over the clattering of beer bottles being tossed into a garbage bag.

"None of your business!" Bryce snapped back. And then, to Thea: "Do they know who?"

Thea slid her phone across the table, no longer able to look at the gummy smile of the familiar man on her screen. A photograph taken on the day he'd graduated. The very same day Thea had.

Bryce's hands rose to her throat as she scanned the picture. "Oh, God. Didn't we go to school with him?"

"George Hegarty," Thea nodded.

"I could swear I saw him working at the bar last night, too. With all the makeup, though… I couldn't tell for sure."

"It says that he worked at the Bloody Mary. You probably did. I… I think I did, too." The smiling bartender dressed as Beetlejuice flashed into her mind. He'd looked familiar. Now, Thea knew why.

"Shit." The curse choked itself from Bryce's throat, mangled and jagged-edged and wrong. Thea didn't know what to do with it. With any of it.

"They're talking about enforcing a curfew until they find out who it is."

Bryce's brows knitted together. "They think it was the same person?"

"Well," Thea shrugged. "We're like the quietest, most crime-free town in the U.S. and then two bodies are found under suspicious circumstances in the same week? It has to be connected, right?"

"Right," Bryce whispered. With a click, she locked Thea's phone and passed it back to her with unseeing eyes. "I guess that means the arcade will close earlier."

"Probably." Another bout of anxiety roiled through Thea, and she tapped an unsteady beat against the table. Even now, she was thinking of all the wrong things, and she hated it. But she didn't have a filter, not when it came to Bryce, so she blurted the ugly concerns aloud anyway. "You know we have to talk about this in the podcast. Everyone will expect us to."

Bryce's focus snapped back to Thea, her dark glare as sharp and cutting as a blade. "Are you kidding?"

Thea wished she *was* kidding. She wished she could be a normal, empathetic person who didn't always have the immediate, relentlessly clawing instinct to figure out why someone was dead before sorrow could even set in. But that was who she was. It was who she'd been for a long time, and it wasn't something she could help.

"No, I'm *not* kidding. We've probably covered more cases like these than the cops have. We can *do* something about this."

"Like what?" Bryce's voice rose and Thea winced. She hated to be on the receiving end of Bryce's fiery ire. "Profiting off people's death? Sensationalizing it for a few listeners' entertainment?"

Thea shook her head, chest heaving with a deep, impatient breath. "That's *not* what this is about. I want to *help*. I think we can use the podcast to do that. We can ask questions, search for answers."

"It isn't our place."

"How different would it be to what we usually do? Why is it okay when we report on a killer from another place, another time, but not one in our own backyard?"

Bryce's lips opened and then shut just as quickly, and Thea knew she'd snared her. People *had* become desensitized to crime and killing, Thea included, but that was who people were. Rather, they could understand how somebody could be so callous than feel the loss and fear that acts of evil left. How could Thea talk about murders each week while ignoring the ones happening in her own town?

"We agreed we'd never romanticize something like this," she said, when Bryce didn't reply. "I'm keeping to that agreement. I know we can do this in a way that's respectful to the victims."

Scratching at her flushed neck, Bryce inclined her head as though weighing up her options. Her fingernails left harsh red lines across her skin. "I don't know, Thea."

"Aren't you the least bit intrigued? The scrapyard thing is so similar to Herbert Humphrey's case. Maybe he has a copycat killer. Maybe *our* killer worked at the scrapyard just like Herbert and we'll be the one to find him out."

"*Them*," Bryce corrected with a sniff of disapproval. "Women can kill. I think about killing *you* almost every day."

"Ha," Thea deadpanned. And then, with the roundest, most

pleading eyes she could manage, she clasped her hands together. "Please?"

Bryce's shoulders slumped, and Thea knew she'd won.

"Fine," she said. "But if we get pulled into any more neighborly barbecues, I'm out. I didn't even get a burger out of it last time."

Thea couldn't help but smile. "Deal."

* * *

It was an agonizingly slow day at the bookstore. Thea might as well have not opened at all, but her mother wouldn't have been too impressed. Fothergill Books had opened at nine and shut at six without fail every day since before Thea was born. Even the day her father had died, Nina had asked her sister, Thea's Aunt Alice, to take care of things while she was called into the station to identify the body. The same went for his funeral. Thea knew better than to break that streak now, even if they had yet to bring in so much as a penny.

Rain was battering the windows outside, which perhaps had something to do with their lack of customers. It felt appropriately gloomy after the news Thea had discovered earlier that morning about George Hegarty. There was something about his death that she couldn't shake from her mind, a weight that hadn't let up since she'd opened the article on her phone this morning. She couldn't identify what it was: maybe the fact she'd known him well enough to copy his homework from him once, or the way he'd been found in a scrapyard less than a week after their podcast about Herbert Humphrey, who'd dumped his victims' bodies in much the same way.

Either way, she couldn't let it go, so she made the most of the quiet moments alone to skim through more articles and scroll through George's social media. The mourners had already flooded in on his Facebook page, a few of whom Thea recognized as old classmates and their parents. It reminded her of how everyone had done the same when her dad had died: people she'd never spoken to before and people she knew he'd hated when he was alive. It made her shudder.

The door swinging open broke her concentration from all of it. She lifted her gaze to find her mother struggling with two bags of groceries, fair hair matted to her face, and her purse sliding from her shoulder to her elbow.

"Mom." Thea sighed, jumping up to grab one of the bags. She left it on the counter for now, but not before glancing through its contents with disapproval. There was enough salad and fruit in here to feed a flock of rabbits. "I told you you don't need to do my shopping."

Nina tutted as she placed the other bag down and wrung out her hair. The rain dripped from her coat and onto the cherry wood floorboards, mascara printed onto her brow bone. "I snooped through your fridge this morning. Microwave meals and leftover pizza is not a balanced diet, Thea."

"The pizza had spinach on it. That's healthy. And I don't need you looking after me. I'm an adult, remember?"

Her mother only cast her an unconvinced look. "I'll believe that when you start acting like one. Have we had many sales this morning?"

"None." Thea slouched and resumed her scrolling.

After shaking off her coat, Nina peered over her shoulder. Curtis women did not know the meaning of privacy, and Thea had long since accepted the fact. She still resisted the urge to hide her phone now, though.

"That poor boy." Nina squeezed Thea's shoulder. "Did you know him well?"

"In passing."

She hooked her damp coat onto the pegs by the door and then tucked her shirt back into her skirt as though that would make up for her sopping wet appearance. "It's awful. I can't imagine what his parents must be going through. I just can't believe this is happening again."

Thea frowned, locking her phone and placing it on the

counter so that she could give her mother her full attention. "When you say 'again', do you mean because of Officer Harmer? Or does 'again' mean this has happened before?"

Nina worried at her lip, regret flickering across her features. Thea knew that look well. It was the look of a mother who'd said something she hadn't intended to, like *I ate your last chocolate donut* or *your rabbit didn't* really *go on a permanent vacation to Hawaii in fourth grade.* "We should get these in your fridge upstairs before they go bad."

"Mom."

She huffed, scraping back her hair so Thea could glimpse every wrinkle in her rain-streaked foundation. Nina was a young fifty, in that she barely looked a day past forty and took plenty of pride in her appearance to make it stay that way. It was times like these, though, that Thea remembered her mother's age, and remembered just how well she knew her. It helped that she and Thea were one and the same, in both appearance and personality. Every mannerism and character trait Thea possessed had been learned from the dainty woman in front of her.

It was because of this that Thea recognized the wave of fear for what it was, when it passed over Nina's features.

"Has it?" she asked again.

Nina bowed her head and nodded. "Once. You were only a few months old, and the town kept it very hush-hush."

Thea's heart began to pound; with dread or excitement, she didn't know. How hadn't she known about this? How hadn't she come across it when she was doing research for the podcast? "Why?"

"Because of the awful state the victims were found in." Nina shifted on her feet, and Thea knew there was more. "And... because the killer was one of our own. Stone Grange's chief of police at the time."

"What?" Thea couldn't get the questions out quick enough. "Who did he kill? How many? *Why?"*

"There were five deaths in total, I think. Honestly, I tried to tune it out. I was a new mom and that was terrifying enough. I don't know much at all."

Thea's brows knitted together, mind racing. It must have triggered a lot of fears that Nina and everyone else in town had long since tried to bury. "Was it printed in any newspapers? The *Stone Grange Gazette*, maybe?"

"Possibly," shrugged Nina. "You could go ask Rita at the library if she has anything in the archives. Just be careful, Thea. There might be a killer around again and I don't want you anywhere near it."

"I'm always careful," said Thea, though she was already itching to text Bryce, get her coat on, and head down to the library to find out more. Stone Grange's very own killer — maybe even two. Could they have been connected somehow?

If they were, Thea would find out. Serial killers were her forté, and she wouldn't let this one go now. She was too close to finding out the truth for that.

* * *

Bryce was thankful that Peter had taken the role of Albert the Albatross today. What she wasn't thankful for was that, with the weather as dreary and wet as it was outside, kids and adults alike had come to waste their Saturday in the arcade. It was chock-full and rowdier than Bryce had ever seen it, so much so that she'd had to call the police station after a group of teenagers had tried prying open one of the coin slot machines to steal the wad of fake fifty-dollar bills stuffed in there. Officer Sara Shaw had responded promptly, and after having reprimanded them with threat of arrest, she now wandered the arcade like a prison warden, looking as restless and glum as Bryce felt.

Thea seemed not to notice any of it when she ambled in just after Bryce's six o'clock evening break to throw an old, soggy pile of newspapers on the desk.

"Oh, God," Bryce grimaced. "Who's dead now?"

"Nobody. Yet." Thea shook out her rainbow-patterned umbrella, the raindrops spraying across Bryce in the process, and then displayed one of the pages in front of her. "I talked to my mom today about the murders. She said this isn't the first time there's been a killing spree in Stone Grange. Did you know about the murders of '96?"

"Here?" Bryce's eyes widened as she inspected the newspapers. The pages were dusty between her fingers, the ink smudged and the edges stained yellow, but she could make out the headline well enough: **'Does Stone Grange Have A Serial Killer On Its Hands? Second Body Found In Woods Outside Of Town. '**

The date listed below was July, 1996. Exactly twenty-five years ago.

"Here." Thea sifted through the pile, opening to another article and pointing. A harrowing mugshot of a dark-haired, cruel-looking and craggy-faced man was pictured beneath Thea's pink fingernail.

'Roger Morris, Stone Grange's Chief of Police, Convicted On Five Charges Of First Degree Murder,' headlined the double page spread.

"How awful is that?" Thea said. "He'd lived here all his life."

"Why don't we know anything about this?"

"Exactly," she smirked. "It was kept on the down-low apparently. The town didn't want it getting out that one of their own had turned out to be a killer."

Bryce's brows knitted together in confusion. It made no sense to her, not really. Every week, she and Thea scoured every database they could for new killers to talk about, and yet one from their own town had gone unnoticed all these years? "Do you think it's connected to George and Isaac's deaths?"

"Doesn't it seem suspicious? The murders *did* start up around the same time of year *and* the bodies were found in similar ways — and a police officer *was* one of the original victims."

"*Squawk!*"

The high-pitched noise gave Bryce a heart attack, and she looked up to find Peter flapping his wings at her side, and a long queue of people waiting to exchange cash and tickets behind Thea.

"Jesus, Peter. Can you not do that right next to my ear? You scared me."

"Sorry." Peter adjusted the beak of the costume so that he could see better and gestured to the customers. "I just thought you should know people are waiting."

"And you couldn't have said that in words?"

Peter shrugged, face gleaming with a light coat of sweat. "Just getting into character."

Thea shuffled away from the desk, taking the newspapers with her while Bryce served the customers. By the end of it, Bryce was sick of the coppery smell of coins and the sound of Peter wishing the patrons a "squawking great night." She was grateful for his help, though, even if he couldn't do much heavy lifting with the gloves on his hands and his tail feather stuck in the slatted vent behind the desk.

"Thanks," she said, when they were done.

"No problem." Peter offered a dimpled, lopsided smile that Bryce knew to look away from hastily or else risk enduring another uncomfortable date proposal. Luckily, Thea returned as soon as they were done and spread the newspapers out again.

"Anyway, I totally think we should talk about this on the pod —"

"*Woah*," Peter uttered. "What's all of this?"

"Keep your beak out," Thea said, only half-joking.

Bryce rolled her eyes at the terrible pun.

"Is it research for the podcast?"

She frowned at that. She didn't remember ever talking about the podcast with Peter. "How do *you* know about that?"

"Are you kidding? I've been listening to it for months. Half of the town has. You guys are famous now."

"You never mentioned it." Thea crossed her arms over her chest, though she wasn't quite sure why it mattered. It just seemed strange that Peter, who was so desperate to talk to Bryce at work that he'd once read out every ingredient listed on his string cheese — a short list to be sure since, shockingly, the main ingredient was cheese — hadn't mentioned to his crush that he listened to her show.

He shrugged nonchalantly. "Didn't I?"

"Anyway —" Thea interjected.

This time, Officer Shaw was the one to interrupt. "What the hell are you doing with those?"

The policewoman nudged past Thea to inspect the newspapers, lips pursed sourly at what she found. "Does Rita know you have these?"

"Yes," said Thea impatiently. "I'm just borrowing them for research purposes."

"You don't think it's a tad insensitive to come in here with them on full display after the town has lost two people this week?" Shaw's cold, grey eyes narrowed. It felt as though Bryce was watching a police interrogation first-hand, or else a woman scolding two badly-behaved children.

"I didn't think of it that way," Thea muttered, as meek as Bryce had ever seen her. "Sorry."

"Put these away," the officer ordered. "Now."

"But Officer Shaw —"

"Thea," Bryce warned, but it was clear when Thea continued that it had fallen on deaf ears.

"Is there anything you can tell us about the deaths? It's just that Bryce and I record a true crime podcast together, and we were wondering if you could give us any information about what might have happened back then."

"Who do you think you are? Velma from *Scooby Doo*?"

Both Bryce and Peter grimaced at Shaw's sharply-spat words. Thea was most definitely on her own on this one. Bryce was almost embarrassed to be associated with her. Her best friend never knew when to stop.

"I lost one of my colleagues this week. Have some *respect*." Shaw stalked off, ponytail swishing behind her as she barged through the customers and left the arcade.

Thea was left to watch, mouth agape, before she turned back to Bryce. "Can you believe her?"

"I know. Clearly, *I'm* Velma. *You're* Daphne." Bryce couldn't help but find some entertainment in Thea's flabbergasted expression. She'd walked right into that one, and Shaw had had every right to scold her for it. Bryce loved Thea endlessly, but she could be insensitive and tactless, and perhaps she needed someone other than Bryce to tell her so sometimes.

"Suspicious, if you ask me. Bad vibes. Maybe even serial killer vibes. I guess we'll soon find out."

Peter spoke up before Bryce could argue. "Wait, you're not *actually* trying to figure out who's killing people in town, are you?"

"*She* is. I'm not," Bryce said at the very same time that Thea proudly announced, "Yes we are."

"Is that a good idea?"

"No," deadpanned Bryce.

Thea shot her a glare. "We know what we're doing."

"No we don't," Bryce mouthed to Peter, before checking her watch. "Anyway, it's time to start closing up. Curfew starts at seven-thirty."

Thea appeared not to have heard her, having a selective hearing problem which strangely only manifested when she chose to ignore whatever Bryce had said. "Did you know either of the victims, Peter?"

Peter snorted beneath his beak. "Am *I* a suspect now? Does that mean I can be on the podcast?"

"Ignore her," sighed Bryce. "I do."

Thea stuck out her tongue churlishly and gathered her newspapers. "I guess no milkshakes tonight."

"I need to go home to make sure Liv hasn't snuck out or stocked the house with beer again, anyway."

"You need assistance?"

Bryce almost wanted to say yes, but Thea didn't always make the whole parenting thing easy. She brought out the child in Bryce, and that made it difficult for her to be the adult figure that Liv needed. That, and Bryce didn't like it when Thea saw that side of her. When she was with her best friend, she could still find some remnants of her fun self rather than the stern, bossy, anxious mother she had to be around Liv. After the mess she'd been last night, she had no intention of subjecting Thea to that again. Perhaps a small, insecure, awful part of her was afraid that if she did, if she kept on this way, Thea would grow tired of her. They were so different in so many ways. How much longer could they sustain their mismatched friendship?

"No, I'm good," she decided finally. "I'll see you tomorrow?"

If Thea minded, she didn't show it. Instead, she nodded and waved, wishing Bryce a goodbye that was not extended to Peter. An announcement from Gus over the loudspeaker rang out above the spilling coins and gaming theme music, alerting the customers to the fact that the arcade was due to close and the police-enforced curfew began tonight. If nothing else, it at least gave Bryce an excuse to get out of work early, though she knew it was selfish to be glad of anything after two people had died.

"You disappeared last night," Peter said, as she began taking down the deflated bags of cotton candy stored behind her.

Right. She'd forgotten about that. "Yeah. I drank too much and Thea had to take me home. Sorry. I was so out of it I didn't even get the chance to say goodbye." It was only half a lie.

"No worries," he brushed off. "Glad you got home okay. I had fun with you, though. Maybe we could do it again sometime?"

She winced. "I think for the sake of my own liver, that wouldn't be a good idea. I have awful acid reflux from those Franken-lime cocktail thingies you kept buying me."

Chuckling, Peter slipped off his albatross hat. Comically, his head looked the size of a pea against the oversized feathery costume body below his neck. "No worries. Message received."

Bryce forced a thin-lipped smile, turning to take the confectionary into the back room, but Peter's voice pulled her back again.

"Hey, Bryce?"

She cocked her head expectantly.

"Is something going on between you and Thea? Are you like… together?"

Heat rushed to Bryce's face, heart plummeting through her stomach, her legs, her feet, the floor holding her up. Why would he think that? Why would *anyone* think that? Had Bryce done something, *said* something, to give people the wrong idea? Had she gone too far? Been too affectionate?

She tried — and failed — to keep her tone neutral as she replied, "No. We're just friends. Why?"

"No reason. I guess I'm just reading into things."

Reading into things. Exactly. Peter was just reading into things. Things that didn't exist.

But as Bryce made her way into the staff corridor, she wondered why her panic had risen so readily if that was true. Had he noticed something last night? Bryce's jealousy when she'd found Thea talking to Heidi, maybe?

It didn't feel like he was just reading into things. It felt like Peter had seen right through the tinted glass wall Bryce kept herself shielded behind. It felt like she'd been put on display, exposed, revealed. It felt like her guard had shattered, walls crumbled.

And no matter how many times she repeated, "We're just friends," to herself as she got ready to leave, it still sounded like a poorly executed lie to her own ears.

FIVE

It felt wrong to sit in the basement and record the podcast the following Tuesday morning, even to Thea. They'd agreed to broach the recent murders with caution, leaving all names out of it and asking that if any listeners had information, they should come forward with it. After that, they fell back into a slightly terse stream of banter as they discussed the horror movies they'd seen that week — a rewatch of *Carrie* for Thea and cult classic *The Lost Boys* for Bryce, which had broken Thea's heart, since Bryce had traitorously enjoyed hot, earring-wearing vampire Kiefer Sutherland without her.

Then they moved onto another true crime story — one that Thea had been dying to talk about for a while now.

"'Our Jane Doe was given the eerie name of the "Lady of the Lake" when she was found drowned on that fateful day in 1977,'" she read from her notes. "'To this day, nobody has been able to identify the body. All that's known about her is that she was a twenty-something woman dressed all in white.'"

"Which is weird in itself," Bryce chimed in. "She was in a summer dress, barefoot, in the middle of a freezing Minnesota winter. None of her other belongings ever turned up, and there was no evidence of assault save for the bruises on her shoulders, which suggested her head was pushed below the water by someone else."

"But what was she doing there?" Thea wondered aloud. "We'll probably never know. It's crazy to think that someone out there might've been the last person to see her alive."

"It's devastating." Shuddering, Bryce sipped her flask of coffee before she continued. "Our Lady of the Lake was buried in an unmarked grave not too far from where she was found. Some of the town members even left fresh flowers for her each year, but I still don't understand how there wasn't one person there who could have helped to identify her. I speak from experience when I say that people in small communities have a way of knowing *everything* about *everyone*."

Thea shrugged, glancing up to find Mikey motioning for them to wrap it up. "Maybe she was a secret agent or something."

Bryce rolled her eyes. "All right, that's about all we have time for today. Next week's episode will be all about a man who was killed by a lethal order of ramen noodles. Make sure you listen and subscribe, and please stay safe out there."

"Bye," added Thea. It was the only thing she could think to say after such a subdued episode.

As soon as Mikey cut the recording, Bryce pouted and slipped off her headphones so that she could press her face to the table without obstruction. "I didn't like that."

"We didn't say or do anything wrong." Thea resisted the urge to reach out for Bryce's extended hand, instead swivelling around on her chair to face Mikey. "What did *you* think, Mikey?"

Mikey lifted his brows in surprise. "You're asking *me*?"

"*Yes*." It wasn't as though Thea and Bryce ignored his very existence. It was just difficult to focus on anything but Bryce sometimes. Too difficult.

"I thought it was fine. You kept it respectful and sensitive."

"Speaking of 'respectful and sensitive,'" Thea ran her tongue across her teeth and wiggled her eyebrows suggestively, "what happened after we left on Friday, social butterfly?"

Cheeks reddening, Mikey scratched the bristle across his chin uncomfortably. "Well… I drank one too many of those green cocktail things and probably made a huge ass of myself. I vaguely remember accidentally dropping a chicken nugget down Hannah's dress."

"Some girls like that," shrugged Thea with as much optimism as she could muster.

"*I* do," Bryce admitted, voice muffled against the table. "As long as I can eat it afterwards. Did *she* eat it?"

"She's a vegetarian."

Thea winced, and Mikey nodded as though to say he'd told her so.

"She should've had Thea's celery sticks instead," said Bryce. "Apparently everyone was saving food in their dresses on Friday."

Mikey raised an eyebrow but didn't ask. Thea was glad. If she talked about Heidi, Bryce would accuse her of liking her again — which wasn't the case. Though they'd had fun on Friday and Heidi was very clearly a goddess sent down from the heavens, she didn't leave Thea with the same depthless flutters Bryce did. Nor did she feel that unbreakable cord tying Thea to Heidi the way it always had with Bryce.

Bryce was special, Thea was beginning to realize. She wouldn't find that same connection anywhere else. Even if it meant a lifetime of drowning in unrequited feelings, Bryce was Bryce. Thea couldn't stop thinking about her, loving her, no matter how many other attractive people she met.

Mikey's continuing complaints broke her from her thoughts. "You shouldn't have left me there. You're sorry excuses for wingwomen."

"*You* try taking care of a terrible teen." Bryce groaned and finally straightened up.

Thea snorted at that, though she still felt awful about Liv and Bryce's argument. "Is she still grounded?"

"Forever. Anyway, Mikey, you should stop pining and just ask her on a damn date. If she says no, then you have your answer and you can move on."

"But... what *if* she says no?"

"Then you have your answer," repeated Bryce, and then shivered as though something was crawling down her back. A spider, or her own experiences with persistent, needy men? "Just make sure you drop it after that. Having to reject a man more than once is uncomfortable for all parties involved."

"Peter?" An irritating flicker of jealousy rose in Thea's stomach, but she *hoped* Bryce was talking about Peter. The sooner she could stop watching him flail and flounce for Bryce's attention, the better.

"Is that the guy you were talking to on Friday?" Mikey flexed his non-existent muscles beneath his shirt. "Do I need to have a word with him?"

"Me first!" volunteered Thea, raising her hand like a school-girl. "There's something... off... about that guy. I don't like him."

"I can't imagine why not."

Thea didn't like the way Mikey smirked at her without subtlety, his eyes glistening as though he knew something she.... Who was she kidding? She knew *exactly* what he knew. It was the very thing she'd desperately been trying to smother in herself for a while now. Apparently, the only one oblivious to it was Bryce herself, and Thea hoped to God it stayed that way.

It was hard, though. It had felt so easy, so *right*, to be with Bryce on Friday; to sleep in her bed and wear her clothes and wrap herself in the coconutty smell of her while their fingers laced together and played like lovers. If Bryce knew, though... Thea doubted things would ever be the same again.

So she ignored it; cherished the few intimate moments she got with her best friend and tried not to let those imposter feelings write themselves all over her face, if only to preserve their friendship. Thea didn't know what she'd do if she lost it — lost Bryce. It wasn't an option.

She glared and kicked Mikey's swivel chair, sending him flying backwards into his computer desk. Bryce seemed not to notice, even with the clatter it made. She was always somewhere else these days, somewhere Thea couldn't reach; always staring glassy-eyed at something Thea couldn't see. It wrung her heart; made it feel like a twisted, damp rag being slowly torn to shreds, but she knew there was only so much she could do for Bryce, and she would do it if she knew what that was. A thousand times, she would do it.

"Bryce?"

Bryce woke from her trance with a sharp intake of breath, twisting a silver ring around her pinky finger. Thea could make out the strip of skin the cheap jewelry had turned green. "I should get going. I have work."

"We'll come with you. Me and Mikey are going to Hannah's store, aren't we, Mikey?" Thea tugged at Mikey's shirt to show he had no choice in the matter.

"Are we?" he groused.

"Yep." Thea beamed and rose from her chair. "We're going to go ask a girl on a date, and apologize for dropping a chicken nugget down her dress, too."

"Great," Mikey said, words laced with sarcasm. "Can't wait."

* * *

Leather 'n' Lace was a small, yellow-paneled store on Maple Street, just around the corner from Fothergill Books. Thea loitered outside, feigning interest first in the wilting pansies planted along the sidewalk, and then the dichotomy on display with the black tutus and biker boots in the window. She could just make out Mikey hovering by the cash register inside, Hannah casting him a dithering look as he no doubt ruined his second chance at asking her out.

She winced when a tray of semi-precious stones he'd had his hands in clattered to the floor by his feet.

"There is absolutely no hope for this boy," she muttered under her breath, watching as he knelt to pick them up. Hannah helped.

But maybe Thea had been wrong, because when their foreheads touched and they both lifted their gazes, Thea could have sworn she saw something pass between them.

It made her heart sing. She wanted that. She *had* that. The way Mikey looked at Hannah now, all starry-eyed and soft smiles, was the way she was certain she looked at Bryce. She didn't want it with anyone else. She couldn't imagine *having* it with anyone else. Even now, standing outside the row of boutiques and bakeries not an hour after Bryce had left for work, Thea missed her. Bryce was the best part of her day.

Thea didn't know what to do about that.

Before she could wonder, Mikey finally emerged wearing a triumphant grin. "I got her number."

"Attaboy!" cheered Thea, dragging him well away from Leather 'n' Lace before he could go back, embarrass himself again, and ruin the entire moment. "I'm so proud. I don't know how the hell you did it, but I'm so proud."

"Thank you." Mikey was almost skipping beside her, which only made it harder to walk linked arm-in-arm with him, not that it was ever easy, since he was six inches taller than her. Now he slipped out of her grasp to coolly adjust the collar of his denim jacket. "It's a new era. I'm a *player,* now."

Thea rolled her eyes and patted his arm. "All right, Danny Zuko; let's not get ahead of ourselves. You have to wait a few days before you ask her out. You don't want to come off too strong." It felt a little too late for that, but Thea didn't want to rain on his parade just yet. "Ask her to get drinks or take her for dinner." She stopped and pointed to a restaurant across the road, where a waiter was setting up the outdoor tables with bunches of artificial sunflowers. "Ooh! Maybe that fancy Italian place!"

"As appreciative as I am for this, Thea, don't you think it's time you started following your own advice?"

A sudden, unexpected defensiveness seized her as she snapped her gaze to him. "What are you talking about?"

"I'm talking about Bryce." He poked Thea in the arm knowingly. "I might be clueless in love, but *you're* not that subtle."

Thea's breath stuttered in her throat, nearly choking her. She swallowed it all down, doing her best to school her composure even as her face prickled with heat. "I don't know what you mean."

"She doesn't know, does she?"

Her expression must have said enough, because a cloying grin curled across his lips as he mussed Thea's braids with a rough hand. "Don't worry. I won't tell her."

"Am I..." Her voice was too hoarse, as though she hadn't used it in months. She cleared her throat and tried again. "Am I that obvious?"

Mikey slung his arms around Thea's shoulders, not to comfort her, but to use her as a crutch as they ambled back down flower-lined, pastel-hued Maple Street. "Not to Bryce, clearly. Why don't you just ask her out? Really?"

A choked scoff fell from her. "Like it's so easy. You get *one* girl's phone number and suddenly you're a love guru."

"That's different. You and Bryce have been close for years."

Too many years. Almost a decade.

"*Exactly.*" Thea squirmed out of Mikey's grip to face him; fear, a cold snake coiling in her gut. "That's why she can never know, Mikey. *Never.* It would ruin everything we have."

Mikey lifted his hands in surrender, his expression crumpling with confusion. "Okay. Okay. Your secret's safe with me. Pinky promise."

He held out his little finger, and Thea hesitated before looping her own around it. "I *mean* it. She can never know."

"Then she'll never learn it from me," he vowed.

It relaxed Thea only slightly as they resumed walking. On the other side of the street, two police officers patrolled; a reminder that there were far worse things happening in this town than Thea's unrequited feelings for her best friend.

"For the record," Mikey said after a few moments of silence, hands plunging into the low pockets of his jeans as he kicked a small, loose stone along, "I don't think you'd get the answer you're afraid of if you *did* tell her. Bryce isn't as subtle as she'd like to think, either."

What did *that* mean? It only felt proof that Mikey was oblivious to the reality of the situation. Bryce was the most guarded person Thea knew; at least, with everyone but Thea. There was no way that Mikey had seen anything between them, anything that meant Bryce *liked* Thea, too. Thea would know. Thea would've noticed.

And yet his words still left hope sparking around her chest like a pinwheel. She tried to douse it in water, tried not to let the fireworks flicker too close to her heart, but how could she?

Bryce was all that Thea wanted; all she'd *ever* wanted, and the only person who didn't seem to know it was Bryce.

* * *

Bryce hadn't intended to open her emails again, but when she'd found Liv's laptop sitting on the coffee table after her shift, well... her fingers slipped. She typed in the password warily, eyes darting back to the *Friends* rerun on TV each time a set of canned laughter erupted, though she hadn't really been watching it to begin with.

Instead of finding Liv's usual Harry Styles screensaver, though, she found a web page already open. The University of California's golden seal was the first thing Bryce saw, and something deep within her stilled. Only her fingers could move, and they took her further down the page, to the course details and tuition fees. A sociology major. It cost more money than Bryce would probably ever earn in her life. She hadn't even known Liv was interested in sociology, *or* Berkeley. All of their conversations about college had been vague, though Bryce had been working hard with the anticipation that once Liv graduated, she would need funds.

But Bryce didn't have *this* type of money, not unless Liv could get a scholarship. She probably couldn't even afford a damn flight to California, let alone everything else that came with college life. How was Bryce supposed to know what needed paying for when she'd never been able to go herself?

"Hey."

Bryce almost jumped from the couch at the sudden interruption. Liv stood at the living room door, a face mask covering her features and a bowl of cereal in her hand.

"Jesus. I thought you were a ghost." With her white dressing gown and goop-slathered face, she *did* look an awful lot like Casper. "Come here."

Liv sighed. "What have I done now?"

"Nothing. Just sit."

Placing her bowl on the coffee table, Liv collapsed with a huff and Bryce pushed the laptop into view between them. Liv's eyes widened when she saw what Bryce had found. "Have you been snooping again?"

"It's not snooping if you leave the page open for me to find."

Clucking her tongue, Liv clicked the page closed and tucked her knees to her chest. "You weren't supposed to see it. You never use my laptop."

"Why do you never talk to me about this stuff?" Bryce was unable to keep the hurt from seeping into her voice. "I'd like to know what you want out of your future, y'know."

"Because you want to get rid of me?" Liv's usual taunting had ebbed to flat words and blank features. Her lips pressed into a pout, shoulders slumped.

Bryce's forehead wrinkled with grave lines of worry, then. "No. Because we're a team, you and me. I want to make sure I'm prepared for whatever you choose. I want to be involved in your life."

"Well, you don't have to worry. I know I have no chance of getting into Berkeley." Liv hauled herself up from the couch, but Bryce caught her wrist before she could walk away.

"Hey. *Talk* to me. Do you *want* to go to Berkeley?"

"No." Liv shrugged, crossing her arms over her chest. Bryce cast her a skeptical look, and she sagged further before throwing her hands up. "Fine. *Maybe.* I don't *know.* It was just an idea. My advisor said it would be worth looking into, that's all."

Bryce patted the space on the couch beside her, and Liv plonked herself back down. "All right. Do they do scholarships?"

"I think so." A scoff, and then: "This is stupid. It's not like we can afford for me to move to California, and my grades aren't that good anyway."

"You must be doing something right if your advisor recommended it." She crossed her legs, determined now not to let this go. "Can we drop this whole teenage brooding thing you've got going on and have a real conversation, please?"

Liv rolled her eyes, and it was answer enough. Apparently the brooding was written in her DNA.

"Why sociology?"

She shrugged. "I think I want to be a counselor or a social worker. Someone who *we* needed, growing up. Someone who helps people like us."

An ache began to swell in Bryce's throat, one of pride and surprise. One of awe. She'd had no idea Liv had thought like that. "I think that's a great idea, Livvy."

"Yeah?"

Bryce nodded, pulling on Liv's damp braid softly. "Yeah. If that's what you want, you have to go for it."

"There are tons of other schools. I could just enroll in some community college nearby."

She heard the doubt, the lack of commitment, in Liv's voice and knew that it wasn't what she wanted. She wanted *Berkeley. California.* And Bryce could imagine her there, studying in the sun and meeting new people, heading down to the beach on the weekend and living a life much less dreary than this one. She couldn't blame her for wanting to get out of this dead-end — and, as of recently, death-riddled — town.

"Why are you holding back? If your advisor says it's worth thinking about, it's worth thinking about. Don't sell yourself short."

"Who are you fooling, Bryce?" Liv's knee jigged up and down as she looked anywhere but at Bryce. "You can't afford tuition or travel fees. We have no savings. I can't just jet off to Berkeley."

It felt like a punch to the gut, knowing Liv had to worry about money. Knowing that their situation was holding her back, making her feel as though she couldn't have the life she deserved. Bryce had worked so hard to fix that, and yet it hadn't done a thing for either of them.

"It's *not* your job to worry about money. It's mine. I'll figure something out. I can work a second job until you graduate and take out a loan."

Liv shook her head. "You already do so much for me, Bryce.

Too much."

Bryce softened, squeezing Liv's shoulder gently. "It's my job."

"No, it's not." Bryce could have sworn she saw Liv's chin wobble. "It was *never* your job. It's not fair that I ruined your life."

Heart wrenching, Bryce shuffled closer to her sister. "Don't be silly. You didn't ruin my life. Why would you ever think that?"

"You were right, Friday night. You just wanted one night to yourself, one night where you didn't have to be my mom, and I ruined it."

"I shouldn't have said those things to you." Her voice grew hoarse, broken, and it took everything in her to keep herself together. God, it was so hard. It had always been so hard. Would she always be this riddled with guilt over every mistake she made? "I was being selfish, and I was angry. The truth is, I could never have a night not being your mom. I worry too much for that. Not because I don't trust you, but because I don't trust myself to get this right. But I swear, Liv, I'll do everything I can to help make Berkeley happen if it's what you want. I made a vow to myself a long time ago that you'd get a better life than the rest of us, and I intend to stick to it."

"I already have a better life." Beneath her face mask, Liv's eyes turned watery. "Because of you."

She crawled into Bryce's arms without warning, and Bryce's eyes fluttered closed against her own tears. "I love you, Livvy. I'm always going to look out for you, even when you're a pain in my ass."

A laugh bubbled from Liv. "I love you, too."

It wasn't easy, this life, but Bryce wouldn't change it for anything. She loved her sister too much. Loved taking care of her, even when it drained her and upset her and made her grieve at all the things she couldn't have. And she would do anything to make sure Liv got the happiness she deserved, so that night, when Liv had gone to bed, Bryce finally called up that months-old email, and sent Genevieve Cox a reply.

Only to inquire, she told herself. Because if she was going to be paying for college tuition and rent deposit and plane tickets and God only knew what else, she'd need any job offer she could get, even if entertaining it at all left a shard of guilt embedded deep in her chest.

Thea would understand, Bryce told herself. She would have to understand.

SIX

Thea rarely saw Mikey in the bookstore unless he was passing through to the basement on podcast days, so when he turned up on Friday morning, wide-eyed and hair a loose nest of straw atop his head, clutching a newspaper, Thea sensed something was wrong. He didn't stop to tell her what; instead giving only a nod towards the backroom before disappearing through it, down, she presumed, into the basement.

She told her mom that she was taking an early break and rushed down after him with her apron still on. When they weren't recording, the dank basement was eerie, lifeless; and Thea crossed her arms to shield herself from the unexpectedly cool air. Mikey stood behind his desk, newspaper sprawled in front of him.

That wasn't a good sign. Nothing good had come out of newspapers recently.

"What is it? What's going on?"

"Where's Bryce?" he asked.

"Here," a rough voice called from the top of the stairs. Bryce made her way down quickly, looking grumpy as ever at being summoned before ten in the morning. She punched a cobweb out of the way on the bottom step just to make sure the spiders knew it, too. "Just to be clear, we're *not* making these early meetings into a habit. You get my *Tuesday* mornings. That's it."

Thea rose to defend herself. "Don't blame *me!*"

"Oh, I don't." Bryce shot Mikey a glare that Thea wished to never be on the receiving end of.

"Hannah is missing!" Mikey bellowed above it all, leaving them both to freeze where they stood.

"*What?*"

"Shit," breathed Bryce at the same time, hunching over the desk to read the newspaper. She showed it to Thea a few moments later, fingers trembling against the bold-type headline.

'Local Girl Goes Missing Days After Second Stone Grange Murder.'

Dread seized Thea's stomach as she eyed the photograph beneath, because she was more than just acquainted with the victim. Hannah was pictured, clear as day, less made-up than Thea was used to seeing her and seeming less than happy to be posing with birthday balloons on her twenty-fourth birthday.

She'd been detached from it before. The victims had been barely more than strangers to Thea, people she had seen in passing or lost touch with. But Hannah... Thea had seen Hannah not a few days ago, cleaning up crystals and gemstones with Mikey in Leather 'n' Lace. And before that, laughing in the Bloody Mary. Alive.

"She never came home from work on Wednesday." Mikey's throat bobbed with grief. The concern in his eyes left Thea feeling splintered and tender. Wrong. "We have to try to find her."

"Mikey." Exhaustion seeped into Bryce's voice, her body language, as she sighed and raked a hand through her still-damp hair. She'd probably been taking a shower before work this afternoon. "They have police for that."

"And look how well they're doing!" He was more emotional than Thea had ever seen him, his entire body quaking with panic. Not the awkward, gangly boy Thea had always seen him as, but a man worried for a person he cared about. They may not have known each other that well, but Mikey had cared about Hannah. Everyone had been able to see that. "Two murders, Bryce."

"We don't know it's connected," Bryce tried to argue.

Mikey scoffed and shook his head. "So when *you* two want to play Sherlock for a bit of fun, it's all good, but when I'm trying to find someone I care about —"

"We'll do it," Thea interrupted, flashing Bryce a determined glance. It was met only with weariness, uncertainty, and Thea felt guilty for it, but she couldn't stop imagining how it would've felt if it was Bryce who'd gone missing. It was too painful to contemplate. "You're right. If we can help, we should."

"Thank you," he breathed. "They're holding search parties all over town, but nobody's found anything yet."

"Do you know where she went missing?"

"Her car was found on the edge of the woods off Vermillion Drive."

It didn't sound good, and Thea tried not to wince. She knew what happened to people whose cars were left abandoned beside overgrown, forgotten woods. She'd done more than enough podcasts about it. "Give me the paper."

Bryce did, sucking on her cheek as annoyance blazed in her dark eyes. She didn't want to be a part of this, and Thea understood why. But Mikey was their friend, and they couldn't sit here and do nothing.

"There has to be some sort of pattern."

A map of Stone Grange had been printed in every *Gazette* since 2007, when Mrs. Walters, a local farmer, had watched her sheep give birth to a set of conjoined lamb twins, which had consequently sparked an influx of tourists. She tore it from the rest of the paper and flattened it on the desk, snatching a whiteboard marker from a mug of pens by Mikey's computer.

"All right. Officer Harmer was found around here." She circled the junction in the center of town, where Thea knew yellow crime scene tape still sullied the local parents' school runs. "Do we know where he was last seen?"

"On patrol not too far from the arcade," answered Bryce, pointing to a couple of blocks down to the short strip of shops, casinos, and the arcade not far from the River Yarn.

Thea frowned as she marked it off. "Wait. Why would you go through the effort of dumping a body in a sewer when there's a river that's closer?"

"Does it matter?" Mikey's face was all shadows and sharp lines in the low light.

"I don't know. Maybe." It did. Thea felt it gnawing at her. She just didn't know why, and they didn't have time to figure it out now. She chewed on the lid of the pen and searched for her next spot. "George Hegarty was found in the scrapyard just outside of town. Around here."

"Right, but according to the article online, he was last seen leaving the Bloody Mary."

Thea circled the spot on Hoover Street, where they had stood only the week before, and then scratched her chin. She was even more bewildered than she had been before. "They're on opposite sides of town to one another. Who the hell drags a body all that way? This doesn't make any sense."

"Serial killers *don't* make sense. If they did, there wouldn't be so many movies about them," Mikey said wearily.

She shook her head and then marked off Leather 'n' Lace on Maple Street, only a hair's breadth away from where they stood now. She did the same for Vermillion Drive, where Hannah's car had been found. It provided absolutely no insight into where Hannah might be. Thea had expected to find some pattern: a crossing of ley lines like in the movies, or some link between street names, victims, but this killer's technique only translated into willy nilly circles across the map. The victims weren't even the same age, the same gender.

"Look at where they were taken, though." Bryce's fingernail danced across each of the circles, the ink bleeding into the thin paper. They were clustered in a triangular formation, the arcade its point and the other two sites the base. "They were all in the center of town, where people go every day. The shopping streets. It must be someone who hangs around regularly. *Someone* must have seen them hovering."

"If they were a stranger, maybe," Thea agreed, and then it dawned on her. "Maybe that's it. It isn't a stranger or a new neighbor, somebody noticeable. It's someone who blends in, someone nobody would think twice about if they passed them on the street. Everybody knows everybody here. Nobody would ever assume someone we've grown up with is a killer."

"And if the victims knew them, trusted them," Mikey whispered, "it would've been easier to have them cornered. Easier to take them."

Bryce pinched the bridge of her nose. "That narrows it down, then."

"Well, it's something," Thea countered. "A start. There's something else, though. There has to be..."

"A sewer and a scrapyard," Bryce rattled off. "What do they have in common?"

Thea pondered it, staring down at the map through narrowed eyes for minutes on end, until the letters blurred and the ink turned tacky beneath her fingers. They were such familiar spots. Places where Thea and Bryce reported victims being found all the time.

Her blood ran cold with realization. Not *all* the time. Not all the time at all. Only within the last few weeks, on the podcast.

The episode before Isaac Harmer's death had been centered around a murderer who'd used the sewage system to dump his bodies. And then the one last week, just before George Hegarty's death; they'd spoken about Herbert Humphrey hiding his victims in the scrapyard where he worked.

They were following the same pattern.

"Oh, God." *It's a coincidence,* Thea convinced herself. *They're going to think you're crazy for even suggesting it.* But her stomach churned, and she rarely listened to the rational part of her brain anyway.

"What?" Bryce asked.

"It's just... it's gotta be a coincidence that we reported the same style of murders over the last few weeks, right? That Harmer and Hegarty were found in the same places days after each podcast aired? It's not like we have that many listeners, so nobody would... nobody would do that. Nobody would copy our episodes. Right?"

She watched as the color leached slowly, first from Bryce's face, and then Mikey's. And maybe it *was* a coincidence. Maybe they were crazy and perhaps a little arrogant for believing someone might be taking tips from *them*. But it didn't feel that way in the basement, staring at a map marked with places where people had died in their own town.

"No," Bryce rasped. "No way."

"It's the only idea we have." Mikey straightened up and then seemed to sway as though he was going to pass out. He didn't, though, his eyes instead locking on Thea's in determination. "This week's episode was the Lady of the Lake."

Thea gulped, feeling an icy rush through her veins as though she had been thrust into a lake of her own. There were two lakes on either side of town. The quietest was north of the river: Lake Nokona. If Thea was a serial killer, she'd bury her bodies there, where the murky waters might conceal it. The other, Lake Tunwall, was the opposite, always filled with visitors and photographers whether rain or shine.

Mikey was right. It was the only lead they had, and Thea would rather go if only to confirm she was wrong than sit back and hope.

"Thea," Bryce pleaded, but it was too late.

Thea had made her decision.

* * *

Lake Nokona was more a swamp than a lake, all boggy footpaths and overgrown greenery creeping into dark, polluted waters. Bryce shuddered as they made their way around it, trying not to remember all of the time she'd spent here as a teenager with people who'd been no good for her. Then, it had been a place for stoners to hang out and blast bad music. Now, it was empty even of them.

They shouldn't have been there. Bryce knew that. She'd tried to talk them out of it all the way there. But Mikey was determined to find Hannah if she was still alive, and Thea was determined to help. Bryce just hoped it was for less selfish reasons than the podcast.

Deep down, though, she knew what had really driven Thea here. She knew why her best friend could never let these cases go, knew why she took it upon herself to try to solve them. They rarely covered unsolved mysteries on the podcast anymore. Thea always needed an answer — because she'd never gotten one for herself.

Her father had been killed on the way home from a business trip after getting caught up in a random shooting. It had happened at some backwater gas station just outside of a sleepy town he'd had no real reason to drive through. Bryce had had some ideas why he'd been there, miles off the usual route from Seattle to Stone Grange — an affair, most likely — but she'd never spoken about it with Thea, and Thea liked to bury her head in the sand and pretend there was more mystery to it, like he'd been one of the victims they talked about on their podcast and not just a man in the wrong place at the wrong time.

A hoarse peal of caws rent Bryce's thoughts, and she startled against the sound. Thea jumped beside her, eyeing the murder of crows fluttering through the leafy canopy above their heads. As though instinctively, their hands found one another's; Thea's clammy and soft against Bryce's. It brought her comfort. Made her feel safe again, even if they *were* searching for what might turn out to be a body.

Ahead of them, Mikey inspected a fallen tree trunk as though it might hold the answers he needed.

"This was an awful idea," Bryce whispered. "We're not going to find anything."

"We have to try." Thea's blue eyes glistened with unwavering determination. There would be no changing her mind now, Bryce knew.

"We should've gone to the cops. This isn't our job."

"And tell them what?" Thea's boots squelched in the mud as she came to a stop, tearing her hand from Bryce's. The absence left her cold. "The killer is using our podcast for ideas? How ridiculous does that sound?"

"It *is* ridiculous. *All* of this is ridiculous." Bryce huffed. "You shouldn't have agreed to this. What were you thinking, telling Mikey that we'll find her? She's probably already dead."

The severe lines of Thea's brows knitted together as she glared straight ahead of her. "I was thinking that if it was you, I'd want someone to help me look for you. I'd want to believe I'd find you in time, no matter what."

The words knocked the breath from Bryce and sent her stomach twisting, heart pounding. It wasn't the same. Bryce and Thea had been best friends for years. Mikey had barely even spoken to Hannah. Anything he liked about her was based on superficial things he'd witnessed from afar.

But it still made Bryce wonder. It still made her ache. It was easy to forget just how much they cared for one another when Bryce saw Thea every day. And Thea was right. If it was one of them, if it had been Thea... Bryce wouldn't be able to just sit back and wait.

She parted her lips to say just that, but the words were lost on her tongue when Thea motioned to something beyond her. "What's *that?* Is that a shed?"

Bryce turned to eye the tangle of bushes, and found that, yes, there was something hidden in the midst of them. *Shed* was a polite way of describing it, though. It was more a ramshackle of rotting wood and broken windows, cordoned off by bramble and half-concealed by crawling ivy.

She frowned. "I don't remember ever seeing it before."

"Serial killer vibes," Thea whispered. "Come *on.*"

Bryce couldn't help but roll her eyes. She was supposed to be heading to work in an hour or two, and she was about to wade through thorns and mud to investigate God only knew what. "Mikey."

Mikey whipped back to them from by the lake, his sneakers caked in ruddy silt. Bryce gestured to the shed, and he followed behind quietly.

By the time they reached the shed, Bryce was riddled with nettle stings and grazes from the thorns. The deep purple stains of crushed blackberries marred her jeans, burrs had hooked themselves into any crevice of her they could reach, and leaves clung to her hair.

"All right," Thea breathed, yanking a less than impressed Bryce out of the bushes by the hand. Mikey stumbled out after her, his foot snared by a raised tree root. "Let's hope Mr. Serial Killer isn't home."

"Again," Bryce reminded, "could be a Mrs."

Mikey brushed past them both to try the door. He hissed out a curse when it didn't budge, and Bryce tore at the ivy to find a rusted padlock bolting it closed.

"What now, Sherlock?" she asked Thea.

Thea scowled at Bryce's sour tone and plucked a bobby pin from her strawberry blonde hair. The braid that had been haloing her head unravelled down her shoulders in shimmering waves. Freed.

Bryce didn't know why the sight left her breathless. She'd always known Thea was beautiful, with her dainty, freckled features and golden hair. Sunlight made flesh. Not like Bryce, who was all darkness, all plain.

She shouldn't even have been thinking of that, she reminded herself as Thea wedged the pin into the lock. It was painful to watch her try to pick it with clumsy fingers, especially knowing that she had never so much as stolen a candy bar before now.

"Give it here." Impatiently, Bryce snatched the pin from Thea's hands. Though her days of teenage rebellion and petty theft were long over, it was second nature for her to maneuver the pin around now. A click, two, sounded soon after, and the padlock popped loose. "My mom taught me *something,* at least."

"She taught you to pick locks?" asked Mikey. *"Why?"*

"In case I ever got arrested and handcuffed." Bryce slapped the rust from her hands before nudging the door open. The hinges groaned, the stench of something damp, something Bryce didn't want to get any closer to, escaping with the shadows.

"So she raised you to be an outlaw."

"Yep."

She raised a foot to step in, but Thea's hands curled around her upper arm, fingers biting into her flesh. Bryce sent a raised eyebrow over her shoulder to find her best friend cowering behind her back.

"What!? We weren't *all* raised to be fearless criminals. I'm using you as my shield."

"It was *your* idea to come here!" Bryce hissed back at her. She was anything but fearless, but her feet drove her forward; fragile, loose floorboards creaked beneath her feet as she took the plunge.

The place was as dingy and riddled with cobwebs as expected, even worse than the bookstore basement, in fact. Weeds crept through the cracked wood with the watery midday light, and shards of glass from a broken window lay scattered on the floor.

But it wasn't empty or unused. Not at all. The walls were plastered with newspaper clippings and photographs. Bryce thought it was just insulation at first, until she saw an image of Officer Isaac Harmer staring back at her from the corner.

A beam of light shone from a flashlight app on Mikey's phone as he skimmed over it all. There were photographs of George, too, and... Hannah, from their social media accounts.

She drifted to Harmer's picture without hesitation, fingers subconsciously reaching out to trace across his warm, creased features. Seeing him, remembering, still left pain stabbing through her. Some of the articles, roughly cut out from the *Stone Grange Gazette*, were new. Details of his disappearance and his murder; his obituary and his accomplishments. Some of them went back years, to the time he'd rescued a dog from an iced over Lake Tunwall and stopped a thief who had knocked over Miss Kelly on the way out of the grocery store.

The collection branched off to the wall adjacent. Bryce followed it, and Mikey's torch followed her.

"Is that Roger Morris?" Thea squinted. The older newspapers sat right at the top, coffee-stained and faded; the same ones Thea had shown to Bryce just a few days ago, though a different print. Roger Morris's harrowing mugshot glared down at them, but that wasn't all. His cruel face sat beside a clipping of a familiar, gangly child sitting on a man's shoulders.

The newspaper caption named her Sara Morris. And the man... the man was Roger Morris, his moustache-framed grin showing the famous gap between his teeth.

"But that's Sara. Officer Shaw. Roger was her dad," Bryce whispered.

"Then it's her," said Thea. "It must be. Maybe she's finishing what her dad started all those years ago."

Officer Shaw was a little stern sometimes, but Bryce had never imagined her a killer. "But why? What's her motive?"

Both Mikey and Thea shook their heads, at a loss. Bryce could only chew on her cheek, deep in thought. Sara *had* reacted strongly when she'd seen them scouring the newspapers the other day. Maybe because the previous killer had been her dad. Maybe because she didn't want to be found out — or already had been by Isaac. But why the other deaths? What was the point?

"Bryce." Mikey's voice shook with urgency, and Bryce whipped around, heart pounding.

And then her stomach turned to water. The opposite wall didn't display Isaac or George or Hannah. It was for *her.* Photographs of her she hadn't known had been taken: strolling out of work with her sweater pushed up past her elbows, slurping on a milkshake at Dina's with Thea, shopping with Liv on Maple Street. This person had followed her in plain sight. This person had documented her life around town.

Why?

If it *was* Shaw, it made no sense. Bryce had only talked to her a handful of times, usually down at the arcade. There was no reason she — or anyone, for that matter — should have a special interest in her.

"These photographs aren't public pics like the others," Thea said quietly. "They're like… stalker pictures."

"Psychopaths often fixate on one person. Maybe… maybe Shaw is obsessed with you," Mikey suggested.

With the foul taste of ash in her mouth, Bryce turned away from the pictures before they burned themselves into her memory forever. "No. This is all just some sick prank or something. I don't have time for it. I have to go to work. Are you coming?"

"Bryce." Thea tried to catch her hand, but she snatched it

away and pushed past them both, gulping down the rotten-smelling air as soon as she stepped outside. Bile rose in her throat, but she refused to let her fears take hold of her now. This was all just some misunderstanding. All of it.

"We have to figure this out," Thea pleaded, following Bryce back through the bramble and onto the muddy path. Mikey trailed behind.

"Put the lock back on the door." Bryce barked out the orders loudly enough that she swore the ground rattled beneath her feet. Maybe that was just the anxiety, though, still vying for her attention, her weakness. "Nobody can know we were here."

She didn't stick around long enough to see if either of them listened. She needed to get as far away from that shed, this lake, all of it, as possible.

SEVEN

Bryce wouldn't talk to Thea about the photographs. Whenever Thea brought up the shed, she either changed the subject or snapped through barbed words that always made Thea recoil. In fact, they'd barely spoken at all since that day at Lake Nokona, and they could hardly report the shed to the police if Officer Shaw *was* the killer, so when Bryce turned up at the bookstore early Sunday morning, before nine a.m. had even rolled around, relief fizzled through Thea.

It was quickly followed by dread, and then, after that, sheer panic. Because Bryce's eyes were red-rimmed, her face wan and fear-stricken. And the *Gazette* was crumpled in her hands.

"No." It came out as no more than a whisper. Because it couldn't be happening again. Because Bryce's face had been pinned next to Hannah's in that shed, and if they'd found Hannah it meant... "No, Bryce."

Bryce only gave a weak nod and laid the newspaper out.

'**Woman's Body Found In Lake Tunwall Days After Disappearance**.'

Lake Tunwall.

Thea had taken them to the wrong lake.

"Read the next page," Bryce said.

Thea did, wetting her fingers to turn over the paper. Her heart turned to lead in her chest.

'**Suspect Taken In For Questioning, Curfew To Be Lifted**'

The photograph of the suspect, a twenty-something man with a buzzcut, struck her cold. It was the guy she and Mikey had met in the Bloody Mary.

"But that's Hannah's *friend*," Thea frowned. "That's Jace.

He…" She trailed off when the memory of his praise echoed in her mind. "He was a fan of the podcast. He even knew who I was."

It made sense now. If Jace loved the podcast as much as he'd claimed, of course that's where he'd get the ideas from. Maybe they'd been wrong to think the killer was Officer Shaw. Maybe Jace had been behind this all along. Telling Thea and Mikey that he was a listener might even have been a taunt.

The caption didn't just label him as Hannah's friend, but her boyfriend. She wondered if Mikey knew. If he knew any of it.

"But if it was him," she wondered aloud, "why Isaac? Why the photographs of Sara and Roger? Why… why *you?*"

Bryce shook her head, dumbfounded. Her fingers trembled where they rested on the counter. "None of it makes sense. I've never even seen this guy before."

It didn't sit right. When Thea looked at Jace, she didn't see a killer. She didn't see anything at all. She drummed an uneven beat with her knuckles, mind racing with too many different thoughts, arguments, reasons why this wasn't right. "With every murder we've ever researched, who's the first to be blamed?"

"The partner. The jealous boyfriend, the abusive husband, the money-grabbing wife." Bryce didn't miss a beat. Clearly, she'd already thought about it too. It was strange, how they could be so in sync sometimes, so out of it others. Strange, and terrifying. Thea worried that one day they'd never find that unison again. That one day, they'd fall out of tune and it would stay that way.

"And yet it rarely ends up being them. They pinned it on him because it's easy. Because the more people die, the more incompetent the cops look and the less the town trusts them. And if the killer *is* a cop…"

"You still think it was Shaw?"

Before Bryce could reply, the door clattered open. Mikey stood on the threshold, his expression blank and his face drawn. He held a newspaper, too, already wilting between his fingers.

Sympathy welled in Thea, and she rounded the counter to pull him into a hug. "I'm sorry, Mikey."

"They think it was that guy," he whispered into her hair,

gripping the back of her shirt. "Jace."

"I know."

"I didn't even know they were together. She never mentioned it."

"Maybe they weren't. Maybe none of this is true."

"She was found wearing white." Bryce's voice was hoarse. Thea pulled away to gauge her expression and found only the telltale set of her jaw as evidence of her distress. Even now, she was trying so hard to hold herself together. Thea would never have that kind of strength. "I wanted to believe it was all a coincidence, but it's not. They're imitating the deaths we talk about on *Perfect Crimes.*

"Mikey," Thea asked, "is there a way to view our podcast subscribers in the area?"

"Maybe. Why?"

"I just... I don't know. It doesn't feel like it's him. I don't know. None of it makes sense."

Bryce bit down on her trembling bottom lip silently, and Thea wanted nothing more than to reach out for her. She was afraid that if she did, though, Bryce would push her away again. With everything that had happened, she'd shut down, barricade herself somewhere Thea wasn't allowed to follow. The fear that maybe this wasn't over, that maybe the killer was still out there and preparing to target Bryce...

Thea hadn't been able to breathe for days because of it.

"There's a way to know for sure," Thea suggested timidly, glancing first at Mikey and then Bryce.

Mikey frowned. "How?"

"The podcast." She felt sick even saying it. But how else could they be sure? How else could she stop feeling as though Bryce was about to be taken from her? "If it isn't Jace and the killer *is* still out there, they're still listening; and if they're still listening..."

"No." Bryce's voice cleaved through the bookstore, through Thea, with its severity. "You've taken this too far, Thea."

"You said it yourself. Jace *isn't* connected to the other victims. It probably isn't him. What do you suggest? Sitting back and hoping that whoever owns that shed isn't coming for you next? "

"No, I don't suggest that. I suggest cancelling the podcast and leaving this alone for good."

The stunned silence that followed smothered Thea. She scrutinized Bryce; searched for any hint that she didn't mean it. All she found was stone cold determination. "You want to stop doing the podcast?"

"Yes."

"So that's *it?* That's the end of *us?*"

"Yes."

"*No,*" Thea refused, voice cracking with strain. She did her best to keep her features steady; a talent that had been learned only from Bryce. "*No.* We can't let somebody ruin this for us."

"There won't be an 'us' left to ruin if we carry on!" Bryce erupted. "And you know what? *Your* picture wasn't on that wall. It's not *your* decision to make. I've spent too long following you around, getting involved in this crazy shit just to please you, and look where it's gotten us. I can't afford to do this anymore. I have my sister to think about."

Thea flinched against the words, each one an arrow ripping through her chest. She was doing this for *Bryce,* because she was terrified of losing her. How could Bryce not see that?

"And what if we're right? What if the killer *is* still out there? Whether we cancel the podcast or not, they'll search for their next victim; which, by the looks of things, is you. At least this way we know we have *some* control over this, some forewarning."

A look of sheer, heart-wrenching disgust flickered across Bryce's face, and it left Thea with a foul taste in her mouth. What was happening to them? The more she tried to cling to Bryce, the further away from her she seemed to fall.

"You really would watch the entire town die if meant you still got to play this *stupid* game, wouldn't you?"

"Is that *honestly* what you think?" Tears streamed freely down Thea's hot cheeks.

"*Guys, please.*" Mikey stepped between them, shoulders

hunched as though he carried an invisible weight. They all did. "Let's not fight."

"I'm doing this because I *care* about you." Thea inched forward, wringing her hands together as though it might make Bryce just *see*. "Because if someone is coming for you *because of the podcast,* I want to be prepared. I want to help. Because I don't want to wake up tomorrow morning and find your face on the front of the *Gazette,* too."

Bryce didn't believe her. Thea could tell as much by the way her nose wrinkled, the corners of her mouth turning down with that same stubbornness she'd always had.

"You're my best friend, B." Thea's voice cracked with the words, because Bryce wasn't just her best friend. She was so much more than that. She was the person Thea would do anything for; the person for whom Thea would fight tooth and nail just to hear her laugh. The person who she would lie uncomfortably still beside for an entire night if it meant their hands remained laced together in bed without disruption, and the person Thea could talk to at seven in the morning, when she woke grouchy and hungover. She was... Bryce. She was Thea's person. And Thea couldn't stand the idea of Bryce not being a person at all anymore. Seeing the photographs in that shed had been bad enough. If something came of them... "I don't know what else to do. What else can we do?"

Mikey sniffled behind Thea, and she felt him shuffle closer, felt his hand squeeze her shoulder with reassurance. "It has to be your choice, Bryce. But I do think there's a method to Thea's madness. We couldn't save Hannah, but neither could the cops. If the killer really *is* out there, and I think we both know they are, the ball's in our court. They listen to the podcast. They mimic the murders you talk about. If we do this right, we can decide how this goes."

When Bryce's face crumpled and she clutched her sides as though trying to hold herself together, Thea's heart almost ripped through her ribcage.

And she couldn't stand there anymore, too far away, too unable to help her, touch her.

But Bryce slipped away before Thea could get close. A muscle feathered in her jaw as she glared first at Thea and then Mikey through a veil of brimming tears.

"I didn't decide any of this." Her voice didn't sound like her own. It was detached, metallic, as hollow as Thea's chest felt. "Do what you want. I won't be part of it."

"Bryce —" Thea tried to plead, but it was too late. Bryce was gone. Thea had lost her.

* * *

When Bryce had ignored three days' worth of Thea's texts and calls, Thea could do nothing but make the decision for herself. Mikey was behind her all the way, as hell-bent as she was to figure out if the killer really was Sara Shaw, and the two gathered in the basement that Tuesday as they had every previous week.

It was strange without Bryce there. Empty.

Thea couldn't help but let her eyes flicker back to Bryce's usual chair, tucked neatly under the table. Her spiral-bound notebook with the rose-gold cover still sat out, brimming with tattered pages stained with her curly handwriting.

A lump began to swell in Thea's throat if she thought too much about it. About Bryce. She didn't know if any of this was fixable. She only knew that she needed Bryce to be okay, and that couldn't happen if Thea's hunch about Shaw was correct.

She *had* to do this. Even if Bryce never forgave her for it, she had to be *sure*.

"All right, I have our list of subscribers here." Mikey stretched in his chair after a final click of the computer mouse. "All one thousand and eighty-nine of them. We've really taken off since..."

He didn't finish that sentence. He didn't need to. Thea had never wanted to profit off of the deaths, but somehow, it had happened anyway. All she could do now was use that to prevent more.

She peered over Mikey's shoulder at the list, watching him scroll through unfamiliar names and faces. They stopped on profiles without pictures to see if their location was listed, but it seemed a lot of their listeners weren't from Washington at all.

Jace's chiselled, pierced face appeared about halfway down, but they'd expected as much. There had been no further news about his charges yet, and Thea still wasn't convinced he'd had anything to do with it.

"If it *was* Jace, and he *is* taking inspiration from the podcast," Thea wondered aloud, "do you really think he'd come right out and *say* how much he loves it like he did? It seems a little clumsy, and this killer is anything but clumsy. Unless he was taunting us. I don't know. None of it makes sense."

"You're right," Mikey agreed, scratching his stubbled chin tiredly. "It's too easy. I don't buy it yet."

They continued on, stumbling across Thea's mom, who'd never listened to a podcast in her life but had insisted that Thea teach her how to "scribey thingy" when they'd first began recording theirs. Dina from the diner was there, too, but Thea doubted she had time in her busy day to murder people in between running the most popular joint in town.

When she found Heidi Godfrey's profile, her stomach barely fluttered, though it *did* lurch when she saw the profile beneath it.

"Hold on." She halted Mikey's scrolling to point to the familiar face. In his profile picture, Peter Keane's shaggy haircut hung low over his eyes, making him almost unrecognizable, but Thea would know that sheepish grin anywhere. It was often directed at Bryce, and it made Thea feel sick, not just because Thea dreaded Bryce ever warming up to him, but because there was something... *off* about someone so relentlessly oblivious. His persistence despite Bryce's rejections, maybe. "That's Peter from the arcade."

"The one who likes Bryce?"

"Oh my God." Memories of the shed, of those candid photographs of Bryce taken all over town, flashed through Thea's mind. "It *could* be him."

Mikey's thick brows drew together. "*Him*?"

"He's obsessed with Bryce."

"So are you. It doesn't make you a murderer."

Thea shot him a glare and slapped him across the back of the head lightly. "There were pictures of Bryce in the shed. That can't be a coincidence."

"Okay, so what about Roger Morris?" His hazel eyes remained quizzical, unconvinced, and frustration began to rise in Thea's throat. Whatever avenue they went down, nothing added up about that damn shed and the victims the killer had taken. "Why would he care about *him* if he's doing this because of Bryce?"

She had no real answer for that, and Mikey took it as his cue to keep scrolling.

"Don't get distracted now. Sara Shaw is the one with the most connections to this..." he trailed off for a moment and then gestured to the center of the screen. "And there she is."

Indeed, Shaw's name and photograph was wedged between the other subscribers. She listened to the podcast. Any doubts Thea had had dissipated instantly. There were too many coincidences, too much evidence.

"Then let's do this." Thea sat in front of her microphone and slipped her headphones around her neck, pausing only when Mikey swivelled around warily.

"Are you sure you want to do this? If Bryce finds out..."

"I'm *doing* it for *her*." It was a mantra she'd repeated to herself over and over again the previous couple of days. She couldn't lose Bryce. She couldn't risk it. "We have to try."

In agreement, Mikey slipped on his own headphones, closing the list of subscribers to make way for the recording software.

"All right. On the count of three." His voice shook, and his fingers, too, as they hovered over the mouse. "Three, two, one..."

The recording began with a click, and Thea sucked in a ragged breath before glancing down at her script. "Hello, you sick and twisted bunch, and welcome to another episode of *Perfect Crimes*."

She paused as usual, for Bryce to chime in with her own

introduction, before remembering the vacant seat across from her. Chest straining with both anxiety and heartache, Thea continued on alone, fuelled by Mikey's reassuring thumbs up every now and again as she told the story of the Railway Murders. They'd taken place in a New England town not a decade ago, carried out by Joe Marlow, an old train conductor who'd hidden the remains of his victims beneath station platforms and across railway lines so the trains would destroy the evidence for him. In fact, the last of the flattened, mangled, fractured bones weren't found until five years later.

No trains passed through Stone Grange anymore, but an old railway line severed the westernmost town limits from Newhalem Creek, a dense and endless cluster of forests and valleys that few dared venture into alone, for fear of getting lost or caught in the strong river currents. It was as good a location as any to find their killer if she chose to turn up.

Though it had been her idea, Thea found herself hoping she was wrong as she continued talking about remains and bones, death and murder. She hoped for the first time that Jace really *was* the killer, and all of this should already have been put to bed.

But it didn't feel that way, so she finished the podcast as steadily as she could and tried not to wonder what trouble she might've just unleashed.

EIGHT

Thea and Mikey had followed Officer Shaw wherever they could since the podcast had gone live on Wednesday morning. It felt as though they were on a stakeout, their days spent sitting in Mikey's car and snacking on Dina's cheese fries while they waited for something to happen; waited for Shaw — or Sara Morris — to scout out her next victim.

Bryce still hadn't reached out, but Thea knew her work schedule and took time out of Shaw-spying, as Mikey called it, to make sure she always got to and from the arcade safely. It was still more than likely that Bryce was next on the list, and Thea wasn't going to let anything happen to her.

By Friday, Thea was jittery, restless, and completely unsure of herself. They hadn't observed anything suspicious or even remotely interesting, her legs were constantly cramping from sitting all day, and she was sick of listening to the same three droning Smiths albums — the only CDs Mikey owned. Shaw didn't start work until noon, and they followed her on her usual patrol around Stone Grange, where she did nothing save for reprimanding a truant high school student smoking pot in the park and an old drunk for urinating in the bushes outside the Bloody Mary.

Things changed that evening, when the sky was a glowing amber and the analog clock on Mikey's dashboard ticked to eight-thirty. Shaw led them in a snaking pattern right through town, towards Dina's Diner. The railway line just so happened to be in the same direction, and Thea's heart thundered the closer they got.

But they didn't end up as far as the tracks. In fact, they rolled to a stop just before them, in the huge field behind Dina's, along with fifty or so other cars parked in crooked rows. Dina stood at the front of the line, handing out tickets and popcorn. A plain white square was projected on the diner's brick wall behind her.

"Crap," Thea cursed as realization set in. "There's a drive-in tonight. I didn't even know."

Mikey shook his head with equal cluelessness as he parked and shut off the engine. His knuckles whitened against the steering wheel. Ahead of them, Shaw had rolled to a stop, too. She'd probably been sent here to patrol in case things got rowdy. It wouldn't have been the first time.

It seemed they'd been led on a wild goose chase just to watch *Breakfast at Tiffany's*.

"What now?"

Thea scanned the lot, focus falling on the thin veil of trees that curtained the field from the old railroad tracks. The weight of what she'd done clawed at her all at once, and she squeezed her eyes shut against it.

"Mikey," she breathed shakily.

"What?"

She could barely muster the courage to look at him. "Half of the town is here... in the place where we told the killer to come. If she strikes tonight, we've baited her into an entire pool of potential victims...

"We've just put *everybody* in Stone Grange in danger."

❊ ❊ ❊

Bryce had thought that after the conversation she'd had with her last week, Liv was done breaking Bryce's rules, so when Bryce came home to an empty house and a note written in pencil that read, *'Gone to the drive-in with Tasha, don't wait up!'* pinned to the fridge by a magnet, she was less than impressed.

Never mind the fact that Liv was supposed to be grounded after the stunt she'd pulled only a few weekends ago, there was also the fact that a homicidal maniac may or may not've still been terrorizing the town. Still haunted by the shed and all she had discovered in it, Bryce had no idea if she believed Jace's guilt or not, but either way, her sister going out just before dark didn't sit well in her stomach, and Bryce ripped the note from the fridge vehemently before setting out to the diner on her bike.

By the time she'd pedalled into the rolling fields, where a colony of cars had flattened the damp grass and left muddy tire tracks in their wake, Bryce was soaked in sweat and her legs were throbbing. Audrey Hepburn's glamorous features flitted across the brickwork of Dina's Diner in black and white, and if Bryce hadn't been so riled up, she might have been sitting here, too, with Thea and Mikey, gushing over her beauty.

But that part of her life was over. Other than a few texts, Thea hadn't bothered to make things right, and Bryce had woken on Wednesday to find a new episode of *Perfect Crimes* available, despite the fact that it had torn their friendship apart.

So, after sending an apologetic glance towards Dina for turning up on a bicycle rather than a car, and for not purchasing a ticket, either, Bryce searched the rows upon rows of vehicles desperately. She ignored the frustrated requests for her to move as she paced each aisle, breathless and not quite sure why she was so frenzied when the rest of the town already appeared to have forgotten the three recent murders.

"Bryce!" a deep, non-Liv voice called. She turned to find Peter throwing a handful of popcorn in the air and catching one lonely kernel as he leaned against his car. "Want to join me?"

Bryce shook her head. "Have you seen my sister?"

He frowned, scratching his head. "No, sorry. Is everything okay?"

"Just let me know if you see her."

Bryce continued the search without waiting for a response and found a familiar face halfway down the lot: the blonde-haired girl, Tasha, who'd slept over in Liv's bed a few times. She lounged on the hood of a beaten Ford Focus with two other girls Bryce somehow knew — probably because they'd brought beer into the damn house the night she'd had blown up.

"Hey, Bryce." Tasha waved gingerly when she saw Bryce approaching, face tinged green with dread.

"Where's my sister?" Bryce demanded, peering through the car's windows to see if Liv was hiding inside. Aside from McDonald's cartons and Dorito bags, it was empty.

"She went to get snacks, I think." The answer was weak, and Bryce crossed her arms over her chest.

"You already seem to have plenty of snacks. Take it from me: If you're going to go the teen rebel route, you need to learn how to lie better."

Tasha sighed and twanged a hair tie against her wrist with trembling fingers. "I think she went off somewhere with Finn."

It took everything in Bryce not to erupt. "Where?"

"I don't know. This is his car so they can't be that far away."

Bryce's fingers flexed with irritation as she wandered away. The place was open, so if Liv was anywhere close, Bryce would have seen her by now. She returned to the front of the lot, where Dina manned a hot dog stall and popcorn machine. "Everything okay, sweet? You hungry?"

"Have you seen my sister around?"

"Not since the movie started." Dina grimaced apologetically. "She in trouble again?"

"Oh, she has no idea. Thanks, Dina."

Bryce continued to search high and low for a familiar head of brown curls but found no sign of Liv. As she made her way to the back of the lot again, though, she *did* find Mikey's familiar Chevy — and froze. He and Thea were visible through the windshield; both of them had already noticed her.

Before Bryce's knees could buckle from the pain of seeing them here together without her, Bryce turned around to head back the way she'd come. Before she could get too far, the sound of a car door swinging open echoed over Audrey Hepburn's softly spoken monologue, and then her name was called.

"Bryce!"

Footsteps squelched their way towards her. Bryce inhaled through tight lungs before whipping back around on her heel. Only Thea had followed; Mikey still sat in his car, pretending that he wasn't watching them through his open window.

"Have you seen my sister?"

Thea's face paled, and it sent a disorienting shiver down Bryce's spine. "Liv is here?"

"Have you seen her or not?"

She seemed to grapple with something, mouth opening and then shutting as her eyes darted around. "No. But she shouldn't be here, Bryce."

"Yeah, no shit. She's grounded — for life, now."

"That's not what I mean."

Her severe tone caused Bryce to falter, and her eyes snapped unwillingly back to Thea. It was hard to look at her after the fight. Hard not to miss her, to wish she could reach out and tighten the scrunchie falling loose from her hair. Harder still because Thea looked as though she was going to throw up on Bryce's boots.

Oh, God. If she was here tonight because of something to do with the killer...

"Then what *do* you mean?" Bryce could barely spit the quivering question out, too afraid of what the answer might be.

Thea played with the button on her dungarees. Her pastel nail polish was chipped and faded, fingers pale and shaking. She never usually left her nails untidy, not like Bryce did. That knowledge alone filled her with dread.

"I didn't know there was a drive-in tonight. *I swear,* I didn't know."

"What have you done?" Bryce could barely hear her voice through the pounding in her own ears.

"We put out the podcast this week. We thought that maybe we could catch Shaw that way, like we planned."

Like you *planned*, Bryce would've accused, had she not been drowning in an icy wave of panic. Panic and piercing anger. "You were hoping to lure a killer here? To a drive-in? Where half the town, *including kids,* are?"

"No!" Thea's brows furrowed desperately. "No, I *told* you I didn't know about the drive-in. The podcast was about the Railway Murders. We've been trailing Shaw all week, waiting for her to

strike. She came here tonight. We think maybe… it might happen."

Bryce had glimpsed Shaw in her blue uniform earlier, and had looked the other way. If she was here, she was here on duty, not to kill someone.

If Bryce responded to Thea, she was worried she might explode, so she marched away before it happened. She couldn't believe it. Couldn't believe that Thea had chosen to throw away their friendship to find the damn killer. Nothing mattered to her but murder and crime. Nothing. Not even Bryce.

Thea followed at her heels as she strode further away from the cars, towards the copse of trees that fringed the field. They were swathed in shadows now, the sky an angry ripple of purple as twilight fell.

Cold hands found Bryce's arm, tightening to try to get her to stop. Bryce snatched it away, lips curling in disgust, in fear, in heartbreak. Her best friend had done this. The woman she loved, trusted, more than anybody. The woman she would willingly choose to spend her life with had she not been working herself to the bone for her sister.

"Please, Bryce. I'm sorry. I'm *so* sorry. I had no idea that you or Liv or anyone would be here tonight. You *have* to believe me."

"I *don't* believe you!" Bryce yelled, and it was true. She didn't believe *any* of it anymore. "I don't believe you care about anybody but yourself. You think you can just walk around playing detective as though people's lives aren't at stake, as though that might bring him back!"

Silence fell with Bryce's words, and then Thea's face crumpled with confusion. "Bring *who* back?"

If she'd been in her right mind, Bryce wouldn't have gone any further. But Liv was missing and Thea wouldn't listen to anything she said, and she was done holding her tongue. "Your dad. That's what this is *really* about, isn't it? You never got over his death. You wanted so badly to believe that it was some great unsolved mystery, so you play with other people's deaths as though it might solve his. We're just your toys. Your way of dealing with grief. You don't give a shit about us."

Bryce saw the hurt dance across Thea's face, but it did nothing to make her feel better.

"Don't bring him into this. I was doing this for *you*. Because you could still be the killer's next target."

Scraping her hand across her tear-stricken face, Bryce shook her head and stumbled back onto the path. "I don't have time for this. I need to find my sister."

"I'll help you."

Bryce didn't want Thea's help, but she didn't have the energy to argue; to think about anything other than the fact that a killer might strike tonight, and her sister was nowhere to be found. And those pictures on the shed…

"Hey!" A voice broke her out of her thoughts as they reached the treeline. Officer Shaw jogged towards them, face twisted with concern. Bryce tried to search for some sign that it was her, that she was the killer, but she found none. She didn't even look like Roger Morris anymore. Not like she had as a child. "Is everything okay down here? You're missing the movie."

"We're fine," Thea said, at the same time Bryce muttered, "I can't find my sister."

Shaw's attention snapped to Bryce, and she tried to ignore the way Thea stiffened. Bryce didn't have a choice. She had to believe Shaw could help. They had no solid proof of anything, and that had to be enough. Otherwise she was on her own, and she was *so* damn tired of being on her own.

"When was the last time you saw her?"

"*I* haven't, but her friends are up there. They said she went off with some guy named Finn."

She must have heard the fear in Bryce's voice, because Shaw softened and squeezed her shoulder. "I'm sure she's fine. I find a lot of teenagers in the old interlocking tower. We can start there."

That was true. Bryce herself had slept in the old, dusty, signal cabin once or twice as a teen, and plenty of kids still played on the bridge and tracks below.

She followed Shaw across the footbridge. Trailing at her side, Thea cast a look Bryce knew well. The 'serial killer vibes' look, all wide eyes and pursed lips. Bryce didn't want to see it. She just wanted to find Olivia. If Shaw threw her sister off the rusted bridge afterwards, so be it.

The tower was half-eaten by overgrown shrubs now, but the door had been left ajar. Bryce nudged it open with the toe of her boot. She'd been praying the whole way here that she'd find her sister, but when she did, straddling the lap of a teenage boy, only anger ricocheted through her.

"Olivia Grace Nicholls. Do you *want* me to haul your ass to a Swiss boarding school?"

"*Bryce?*" Liv stumbled off the sandy-haired boy Bryce could only assume was Finn, straightening out her bunched sweater breathlessly. They were barely more than silhouettes in the dark.

"I'll leave you all to it." Shaw ducked out with a grimace, but Bryce barely noticed.

She didn't have it in her to scream. She didn't have it in her to do anything. Liv clearly wasn't in the business of listening to a word she said. "What part of 'grounded' didn't you understand?"

"Oh, come on, Bryce." Liv sighed, getting to her feet. Her hair was ruffled untidily, lips swollen and cheeks flushed. "We've had curfew for over a week. This is the first time I've been out in ages."

"And I see you used the opportunity wisely." Bryce scowled at Finn, but even that drained energy she no longer had. "I was worried sick about you. Go back to your friends before I drag you home myself."

Liv's forehead wrinkled in confusion. "That's it? No shouting? No lecture?"

"Would you listen if there was?" The question was hollow, as though she'd been wrung out of any emotion, of anything at all. She was cold and exhausted, having worked overtime and double shifts to earn more money to go towards Liv's tuition. She'd lost her best friend, lost her podcast. Found out someone linked to the murders had been spying on her. It was too much. She could only build a sharply-pointed fence around herself to keep it out, to keep anything from touching her — even Liv. Because if it did, if she thought about it for too long, she would finally break.

"I'm sorry."

"No, you're not. Just go back to the movie, Liv. Please. We'll talk about it later."

"Bryce," Liv pleaded. "Are you okay?"

She wasn't okay, but Liv didn't deserve to bear the brunt of it even now. So Bryce nodded, chewing on her bottom lip and gesturing to the bridge. "Just go."

Head bowed, both Liv and Finn brushed past her. Bryce watched as their figures retreated safely across the footbridge and began the hike back to the field, and readied herself to follow. Warmth at her hands stopped her. Thea had interlaced their fingers and looked at her with watery, concerned eyes that Bryce found it hard not to crumble beneath.

"I'm sorry, Bryce," Thea whispered. "I'm so, so sorry."

Bryce's chin wobbled. She gritted her teeth to steady it. *No. Not now. You've managed this far.* "Still think it's Shaw?"

"I... I don't know *what* I think anymore. I just wanted *you* to be safe. Maybe you're right." Tears spilled over Thea's cheeks, and Bryce couldn't look at her anymore. It hurt too much to see her cry. "Maybe all of this *is* just an obsession left over from my dad's murder. I guess that makes sense. I just wanted answers. I just wanted you to be safe. If someone hurt you the way they hurt him..."

Thea's voice broke, and Bryce winced against it. She hadn't thought of it that way. She hadn't known Thea's loss could ever extend to Bryce, too. "*You* hurt me, Thea."

"I didn't mean to. I swear I didn't mean to. You're right. I was fucked up. I made such a mess, and none of it was worth losing you over. None of it." Thea gathered Bryce into a tight hug, and Bryce didn't have it in her to pull away. Despite everything, this was still the only way she could ever feel safe: with Thea. And she knew that, awful as it was, this was just another way Thea had thought she was taking care of Bryce. She was always doing that: taking care of her. *Someone has to.*

She let herself relax when Thea's hands tickled the nape of her neck and then ran soothing circles across her back. "I love you,

Bryce," she muttered into Bryce's shoulder, clinging on to her as though for dear life. "I love you. I'm so, so sorry."

"I'm sorry, too," Bryce admitted. "I shouldn't have brought up your dad."

"You were right."

"I was being cruel."

"You deserved to be. Look at what I've done to us." Thea pulled away only slightly, and Bryce felt the tears she'd left behind dampening her shirt. She knew, then, that this was why they would always make sense, and why she could never stay mad at Thea for too long. Because Thea had seen Bryce at her worst and was still here. And Bryce could only return that same courtesy.

They would always be there for one another. Always. Nothing could ever drive them apart, not even each other. Not even their ugliest sides. Because even then, even when it hurt, it was all driven by their love for one another.

And Bryce *loved* Thea. She loved her more than anything, save for her sister and maybe Neve Campbell. Thea was the only thing Bryce chose every single day, and she would keep choosing her. She couldn't remember it being any other way, and it wasn't something she could unlearn or run from.

She longed to be closer to Thea, still. She wanted to feel her warmth, have her close enough that Bryce wouldn't be tempted to push her away again, so she let her forehead rest against Thea's, listening to the way her chest heaved with suppressed sobs as Thea's soft hands found her jaw.

"I love you," Thea whispered again, though she didn't need to. Bryce could feel it as well as she could feel her own heart beating. "I'm so sorry."

She didn't know how their lips fell together after that. She didn't know how it hadn't happened sooner, either, as weightless warmth blossomed through her. There was nothing but Thea and the taste of mingling, salty tears, and the way Bryce felt about her, as though she never wanted to let her go. She had thought that a love like this would make her ache, but here, now, she couldn't imagine it ever aching. It was the only thing in her life, perhaps, that didn't hurt at all, and Bryce chose to let it in, chose to let herself be vulnerable to it, *her,* as the kiss deepened and their noses brushed.

She'd been worried that the jealousy she'd felt not too long ago might break them if she let herself feel it, because friends weren't supposed to be jealous, weren't supposed to feel too much. But there was no danger of that now. They were here, together, and nothing was breaking or hurting or wrong. Nothing would ever break them.

For the first time in Bryce's life, the shadows couldn't catch her. Thea had chased them all away.

NINE

Thea's lips, her bones, still hummed from kissing Bryce as they made their way back over the tracks, boots clanging against the metal walkway of the bridge. She didn't know where the kiss had left them. Bryce hadn't said. She hadn't said much of anything at all, though her hand remained locked in Thea's. Thea wanted to ask, but she didn't want to push her. Not tonight. Not after everything she was already going through.

"There's something I have to tell you," Bryce whispered, coming to a stop halfway across.

"Okay." Thea's heart raced — with anticipation and with dread. She tried to convince herself it would be good; that Bryce was about to tell her everything Thea had ever wanted to hear, and not that she already regretted the kiss.

But then the corner of Bryce's mouth tugged down, and the panic set in, and Thea couldn't look at her as she waited for Bryce to deliver her blow. She scraped the loose strands of her hair back against the wind, bracing her elbows on the icy, steel railing, and let her gaze fall to the endless tracks ahead. Riddled with all sorts of debris — scrap metals, charred wood from campfires, a shopping cart, — they bled into a stagnant, smothering darkness eventually. Absently, Thea wondered just how far they'd take her if she followed them.

"I got this email a few weeks ago..." Bryce began.

Thea wasn't listening, though. She'd frozen completely at the sight of a shadowy heap below them, sprawled across the old, slatted tracks. "Bryce. Look."

She did, their arms brushing as Bryce joined her to peer over the railing. Confusion flickered across her features, and Thea wondered if she was imagining it — if that heap *didn't* look like a body — but then Bryce's lips parted and her grip on the railings tightened and Thea knew.

"Shit."

"Go find help," Thea ordered, already jogging towards the steps on the other side of the bridge. "I'll go see who it is."

It wasn't Liv. The body was too long, too large against her petite frame, and that knowledge at least calmed her enough to think logically.

"Wait." Bryce tugged at Thea's wrist, throat bobbing as she swallowed. Her eyes sparkled with fear, panic. "Be careful. Have you got your keys?"

Thea frowned. "Yeah, but..."

The argument was lost on her tongue. Bryce rifled through Thea's pockets as comfortably as though they were her own, drawing out Thea's set of apartment and bookstore keys, complete with fluffy, pastel pom poms and a crocheted pansexual flag Bryce had bought her after she came out a few years back.

"Hold them like this," Bryce instructed, as she dug out her own keys and slid her middle finger through the split ring. She closed her fist so the pointed tip of her house key protruded between her first two fingers. "I'll be quick as I can. Are you sure —?"

"Just go!" Thea instructed, urging her forward. Bryce shifted hesitantly, features strained, and Thea could see the war within her. But they didn't have time for more arguments, and Thea couldn't worry about anything but the person lying on the tracks. "Go, Bryce."

"Quick as I can," Bryce vowed again, and took the pathway back to the field, back to Dina's. Thea could only hope help wasn't too far away as she hurtled down the steps two at a time, heart racing and palms slick with sweat.

"Please don't be a dead body," she pleaded aloud, breathless and trembling as her Vans met with the gravel and slatted wood. She stumbled her way across the tracks, to the dark heap in the center. It hadn't moved. *They* hadn't moved.

Fear twinged through her as she examined the limp body,

recognizing the navy police uniform almost immediately. Sara Shaw lay still below Thea's feet, eyes closed and a deep gash leaking blood from her temple.

"Oh no. Oh no, oh no, oh no."

Thea had been wrong, she realized, as she shook Shaw's shoulder in an attempt to wake her. Shaw *wasn't* the killer — or, if she was, she wasn't a very good one to have been assaulted, herself.

She checked her pulse when Shaw didn't respond; found a flutter in her wrist that provided little relief. Her chest still rose with breaths, too, but the rest of her...

Her legs looked twisted, and Thea blinked up toward the bridge, wondering if she'd been pushed. It was a survivable height, Thea guessed, but she wouldn't have liked to take her own chances on such a fall.

"Officer Shaw," she tried again desperately, shaking more carefully now. She wanted to roll her into a recovery position, but had no idea if it was the right thing to do after a fall. If her bones were as fractured as she looked, it didn't seem a good idea.

With trembling fingers, she reached into her pocket for her phone. As she did, Shaw began to stir, a low groan coming from her as her face wrinkled with pain.

"Officer Shaw?"

The name finally garnered Shaw's attention, and the officer's eyes rounded with fear as she clutched Thea's arms. "Thea. Be —"

Thea would never learn what Shaw had been about to say. A sharp, nauseating explosion of pain sang through her skull, and Thea collapsed beside Shaw. A stony-edged darkness began to blanket her — her last thought, that Bryce was probably looking for Shaw.

But Shaw was already here.

* * *

Bryce couldn't find anybody to help. She spent ten minutes looking for Officer Shaw or an off-duty doctor, anybody who would know what to do, before her fear of leaving Thea alone left her so breathless that spots danced across her vision, and with a final glance across the lot, where everyone still sat watching the show — including her sister and Mikey, thank heavens — she returned to the railway tracks on unsteady feet.

Her heart plummeted to her stomach when she found neither the body nor Thea anywhere on the tracks. Only a smear of blood remained, and she selfishly prayed it wasn't Thea's.

"Thea?" Bryce shouted, panic simmering in her voice as she searched the shadows desperately. *"Thea!"*

"Bryce!" The muffled response wasn't that far away, but Thea's voice sounded mangled and wrong and it only added to Bryce's all-consuming fear. It seemed to drift from somewhere over her shoulder, and she whipped around, eyeing the bushes and fringe of woods for Thea's pale face. She found it by the green metal of the bridge's beams, streaked with tears and covered by a sickly white hand.

Its owner stood above Thea, silencing her by clutching her body tightly to theirs. Bryce's heart stuttered when she saw that the other hand clutched a silver blade against Thea's throat. It winked wickedly in the broken moonlight.

And the person holding her, the person hurting her...

"It was *you.*" Bryce's voice was serrated from the screams that had already left her throat. "It was *all* you."

"It was me." Peter stepped forward, dragging Thea with him. Sweat matted his dirty blond hair to his forehead, and something wrong, something inhuman, twinkled in his pale eyes. "Surprise, Bryce."

She caught another silhouetted, motionless body twisted in the underbrush beside the tracks, but Bryce couldn't make out who it was from here. She couldn't focus on anything but Thea's teary, fear-filled eyes and the sharp knife at her neck.

"Why?" Her voice broke with the question. Peter had been irritating and persistent and a little too eager to get Bryce's attention, but he had never been… *this.* Threatening. Murderous. *Evil.* She'd never thought him capable of it. Of harming somebody. Killing them. She vaguely recalled him refusing to step on a spider in the arcade's cafeteria once.

"You wouldn't notice me any other way," he shrugged, as though it was all casual conversation. "I knew this would make you happy."

Acid rose in her throat at that, her face twisting with disgust. "Most men buy women flowers or chocolates when they want to be noticed, Peter. They don't *kill* people."

"Well, I'm not most men," he sniffed, "and you're not most women. You're *into* this, aren't you? C'mon, Bryce. I've heard the podcasts. You *love* it."

"You're sick," she spat. "Let Thea go."

"So you can leave me for *her?*" He was unhinged… Bryce saw it not just in his words, but the way he looked at her — a predator hell-bent on hunting its prey. His eyes kept her locked in place, saucer-like pupils turning them near-black.

She couldn't move. She couldn't breathe. She had no idea how either of them were going to get out of this. It was clear enough that Peter wasn't about to listen to reason.

"No. No, just *please* let her go."

"How about a compromise, Bryce?" He kicked Thea to the floor with a grimy boot, eliciting a shrill whimper from her. Bryce winced against it. *No.* Bryce had just gotten Thea back. She wouldn't let him hurt her. "I'll save her until last. You can watch me end Morris, first. You'd like that, wouldn't you?"

Peter stepped backwards as he spoke, reaching down to pull the other body up by a fistful of their navy shirt. Bryce winced when she got a good look at Sara Shaw. Her eyes were hooded and her posture limp as though she was only half-conscious.

"Wait," Bryce begged when the knife found Shaw's collarbone, as she choked back a distorted sob. Bryce had to keep him talking, *had* to keep him distracted. "Wait. Tell me *why*, first. I want to know why."

"*Why?*" Peter cocked his head, gritted his teeth, as though the question fuelled him with rage. How unreasonable of Bryce to ask.

"Yes. Why?" Uninvited tears splashed across Bryce's cheeks. She couldn't look at Thea, still kneeling halfway in the bushes. She would break if she did.

"I'm disappointed, Bryce," he sighed. "But it's okay. I'll clue you in. Sara here is Roger Morris's daughter. I thought you'd figured that out after you found my little hideout."

He'd known. He'd known Bryce had been in there, seen his secrets. Even then, he'd been watching her somehow. Waiting to strike. Waiting for this. "And what has Roger Morris got to do with any of this?"

"The son of a bitch killed my mother." Peter's shoulders squared with a sudden, unexpected, fiery fury, and Bryce's breath caught in her throat. She had been so focused on Morris and Shaw, she hadn't even looked at the names of his victims. "When I found out his daughter still lived, I wanted payback."

"But you started with Isaac Harmer. *Why?*"

"It was punishment. Harmer was completely incompetent at his job. He waited until it was too late to catch Morris. He *worked* with the guy and still didn't realize it was him. My mom was dead and buried by the time he finally put Morris behind bars."

"Okay," she nodded, trapping down any defence for Isaac she wanted to let out. She didn't know enough about Morris's case to argue. "What about George Hegarty? What did *he* have to do with it?"

"Nothing. He was just convenient. A new victim to get your attention." Peter's nose began to run, and he wiped it with his sleeve like a toddler who hadn't discovered hankies yet. The knife glinted with the movement, a stark reminder against the night's blackness. "I saw him looking at you in the Bloody Mary, and he was easy enough to get to."

It made no sense — but then, killers didn't make sense. Not to anyone but themselves. Bryce had long since learned that. Whatever Peter's obsession with Bryce had become, it had clouded everything. It made her sick that, in some twisted way, it had been for *her.* As if she could *ever* want this.

"And Hannah?"

"She was your friend. I knew you wouldn't be able to resist investigating. The closer the victims were to you, the closer you got to finding me. Our little game, Bryce. That's what it was, wasn't it?"

Hannah had barely been an acquaintance, but it wouldn't have mattered. Peter had struck where he wanted to, and it had all boiled down to the same outcome; here, now, in the end. He'd wanted Bryce to find him out, to play his sinister game of cat and mouse — had probably expected her to praise him for it.

"I was leading up to the main event," he continued. "The grand finale. Your producer was supposed to be next. Mikey, is it? And then to finish, Thea, and Morris' bastard daughter. Two birds with one stone."

"And *then* what?" Bryce asked. "Is it my turn? Are you going to kill me, too?"

"Your turn?" Peter's brows lifted in surprise. Shaw slumped to the ground as he loosened his hold and stumbled forward, until he stood mere inches away. The knife remained clutched at his side, its tip pointed to the ground. "I thought you were a horror fan, Bryce. You should know you're the *final girl* — and the final girl *always* survives. I did this for *you.* Because I know how much you love it. You said so on the podcasts."

She scoffed, though it came out more of a sob.

Sudden movement distracted Bryce, then, a moving shadow just behind Peter. She jerked her gaze back to him when she realized it was Thea, gesturing with her finger and mouthing something. *Keep him talking.* She was hunched over, extracting a loose plank of wood from the debris among the tracks, and Bryce understood. The idiot had his back turned to an avid horror fan. Rookie mistake.

"I should thank you, then, should I?" Bryce inched backwards, fighting to keep her eyes on his, baiting him to follow. It pulled him further away from Thea and Shaw, who seemed to be clawing up into a sitting position now.

"Exactly." Peter seemed to soften, his eyes slipping to Bryce's lips. "It was all for you, Bryce. You're my final girl."

It made her stomach churn to hear it, but Bryce pasted as believable a smile as she could muster on her lips. "I understand now."

"I knew you would. I've been waiting for you to."

If Peter hadn't been gazing at Bryce with the gleaming, unadulterated infatuation she'd always been too blind to notice before, he might've noticed Thea stand up with the wood in her hands. He might've noticed her step closer, the stones scraping beneath her feet. He might have noticed her struggling to raise it above her head. He certainly noticed as she brought it down, directly onto his skull, sending him sprawling to his knees. Bryce didn't want to waste the opportunity to strike a blow for herself, so she threw all her trembling weight into a final, rough punch across his face, leaving an angry red bruise.

Peter fell, limp and bloody, where he jerked spasmodically on the gravel once, twice, then didn't move again.

"This isn't the Nineties, Peter," Thea said, dropping the wood and slapping her filthy hands together. "There can be more than one final girl."

Relief gusted through Bryce, and she gathered Thea into her arms desperately.

"Are you okay?" Bryce cradled Thea's jaw, her neck, any part of her she could, examining the blood congealed in her hair and the welt on her chin.

"I'm okay," Thea confirmed, brushing Bryce's tears away with the pad of her grubby thumb.

"And I'm okay, too, thanks," Shaw grumbled faintly from the underbrush, flinching as she reached for her radio. Bryce swore at the state of her, all bruised and broken, and dragged Thea towards her so they could help. The radio crackled as she held down the call button, her face an unpromising, waxy shade of green. "This is Officer Shaw. I need urgent police and medical assistance down by the railway overpass behind Dina's. Over."

Another, male, voice rattled back across the line, but she

seemed not to be listening anymore. Her eyes were glassy as she eyed Peter's still body across the tracks. "The secret's out, huh?"

"We already knew about Morris," Thea admitted meekly. "We sort of thought you were the killer until half an hour ago... sorry."

Shaw seemed not to have it in her to even be surprised. "I can admit I'd make a decent suspect. I changed my name because I didn't want to share anything with that monster, though. It must have taken some digging for him to find me out."

Bryce didn't know what to say. She kept waiting for the next trauma, the next tragedy, the next death, like the part in every slasher movie where the killer woke for one last hurrah. But Peter remained splayed out on the tracks until the red and blue lights dappled through the treeline, and paramedics and police emerged across the shrub-invested banks.

Thea's hands brushed Bryce's as though asking if she was all right. She wasn't, but she was at least better when she intertwined her fingers with Thea's. Thea's head fell to Bryce's shoulder with exhaustion, and Bryce could only press one kiss into her blood-spattered hair before they were sucked into the chaotic aftermath — police reports, paramedic checks, trying to explain something that didn't yet make sense to Bryce.

But it was over, she knew as her eyes flickered up to the wispy night sky. It was over.

※ ※ ※

Thea was still numb from everything that had happened. They'd taken her to the hospital for an X-ray and stitched up the wound still throbbing on the back of her head. Mikey had joined her, furious that he'd been too mesmerized by Audrey Hepburn to notice Thea and Bryce trying awfully hard to not get killed. He paced now, from bed to the window and back again, as though not sure it was really over.

It felt over to Thea, more so when Bryce peeked her head

around the blue curtain. She'd taken care of Liv before meeting them here. What that entailed, Thea didn't know. As for Shaw, she'd been carted off with the ambulance engines blaring almost immediately, and Thea had no idea when she'd next see her. Peter, too. She hoped in his case, the answer would be never, though she wasn't ready yet to live with his death on her hands, self-defence or not.

"Is that orange juice?" Bryce's still shaking fingers found the juicebox on Thea's table and sucked on the straw.

Thea raised her eyebrow. "It's *my* orange juice. *I'm* the sick patient."

"I need the sugar before I pass out," Bryce retorted through a slurp, and then set it back down before perching on the edge of Thea's mattress. "How are you feeling?"

"Like I was hit in the head with a large rock." Which was, in fact, what had happened. She'd woken to nettles and brambles and Bryce calling her name. It still felt surreal. All of those murders she'd researched for the podcast, and now she'd survived her own story. She didn't know if she could ever go back to that; she only knew that her perspective on everything had changed and she would find much less excitement in trying to understand killers now. It turned out there was little there to understand. Peter had been unhinged; so lost in the grief of his mother and his obsession with Bryce that he'd turned into a monster.

At the reminder, Thea reached for Bryce's hand and squeezed it, her dirt-caked thumb playing with the cool bands above Bryce's bloodied knuckles.

"I'm going to leave you two alone for a while," Mikey said. He *did* have some social awareness, it seemed.

"Can you keep Liv company in the waiting room?" Bryce requested hopefully.

Mikey only saluted and made himself scarce.

"I'm sorry, Thea," she began a moment later, watery, swollen eyes falling to her unlaced boots. "I'm so sorry."

Thea frowned. "For what?"

"For Peter. For all of this. I blamed you for luring a killer to the drive-in, but it was *me*. It was me he wanted. He would have killed you."

Thea blinked, bewildered. "You can't really think this is *your* fault."

The tears rolling down Bryce's cheeks said otherwise, and they caused something vital in Thea's chest to crack. It always did when Bryce was hurting, as though her pain was Thea's, too. She struggled up from her pillows to embrace Bryce.

"I should've realized it was him," Bryce said.

"You couldn't have known," Thea countered softly. "None of us could've known." It was true. Thea's jealousy had been the only thing driving her distaste for Peter. The only moment she'd questioned his character, when she'd seen him among the other podcast subscribers, had been clouded by her doubt just as quickly. Because even then, she'd only thought him a slightly irritating man who liked Bryce. A thorn in Thea's side. Not somebody capable of killing.

Thea leaned back, Bryce's hair tangling in her own as though it was trying to keep them close. Bryce didn't move back to her end of the bed. Didn't take her hand from Thea's. She hoped Bryce would stay here, wanted to feel Bryce's warmth singing through her blood. Tonight had only cemented what Thea felt. Bryce had been strong and protective and Thea had never felt more fear than when she'd seen Peter close in on her. She loved Bryce. She would never stop loving Bryce.

But she still didn't know if any of it was requited.

"You wanted to tell me something," Thea muttered. "On the bridge, before…" She didn't need to finish *that* sentence. "You said you had something to tell me."

Bryce shook her head. "It doesn't matter now."

"It does," Thea pleaded, if only to know once and for all where she stood. "It matters to me."

Shifting her weight uncomfortably, Bryce pulled one leg onto the bed, dirtying the white sheets with her muddy boot in the process. "I was going to tell you that I got an email from someone who works for Horror Town Studios. She listened to our podcast and asked me if I was interested in presenting a crime documentary. But it doesn't matter now, Thea. I don't want to do anything to jeopardize..." her eyes slid between them uncertainly, "us."

Confused, Thea inched nearer until her thigh brushed Bryce's knee. "Why would that jeopardize us?"

"Because she only asked me. I... I emailed her back because Liv wants to go to Berkeley and I don't have nearly enough savings for that, but I can find another job and I can take out a loan. We can find something together, maybe. Something bigger than the podcast."

Her heart panged at that. Bryce was willing to risk the opportunity of a lifetime and the financial security she'd always been desperate for... for Thea? Thea didn't deserve that. She didn't deserve Bryce — and more than that, she didn't want to watch Bryce miss out on something wonderful for her own benefit.

"Are you *kidding?*" Thea swiped Bryce's hair from her eyes so she could see her properly. Her hand didn't fall back to her lap, instead resting in the whorl of her chin. "Bryce, you deserve this more than *anybody.* If you have a chance, you have to go for it. It won't change anything between us."

Surprise danced across Bryce's solemn features. "But we started this together."

"And we'll end it together," Thea whispered. "I'll still be there on the sidelines, cheering you on. Always. How could I not?"

Bryce's lips parted, but no words came out.

Thea shook her head at her best friend's selflessness, wiping an escaping tear from the corner of her eye with a delicate, trembling thumb. "You've struggled for so long just to get by, B. I would never want you to sacrifice anything for me. You're always looking after other people, always looking after *me.* Look after *yourself,* now."

They were so close now that the tips of their noses grazed. Bryce's was pink from crying, her face blotchy — but still beautiful, and still Bryce's, and still everything that Thea adored in the world. And she knew that it was now or never. She knew that this was her chance, and if spilling her heart now would end in them drowning, there would still be some way of salvaging it. Together, they could get through anything. Even an intense, unwavering, potentially unrequited love.

So Thea blurted the truth without any of the fear that had plagued her for years. "I'm in love with you."

Bryce stilled beneath her fingertips, dark eyes flickering to meet Thea's.

"I'm in love with you," Thea repeated, if only to fill the stifling silence. "And not in a best friend way. In a 'my heart bursts open every time I see you' way. In a 'if you killed someone, I'd help you bury the body' way. Is that too soon? Let me think of another analogy. In a —"

Bryce's lips swallowed whatever babble Thea was going to continue on with, leaving Thea breathless and safe and yet somehow on fire. She lost herself to the flames, lost herself to all of it. The beeping of heart monitors and the squeaking of nurses' rubber shoes across the linoleum, the clinically bright lights overhead, Thea's tender wound at the crown of her head — they all became secondary. As long as Bryce was here, she could survive anything.

She *had* survived anything. For Bryce. For this.

"I'm in love with you too." Bryce's bottom lip grazed against her teeth in a way that left Thea trembling. "And not in a *friend* way."

It was everything Thea had ever needed to hear, and she smiled into her next kiss, and all the ones after. Because somehow, against all odds, Bryce loved her back. Her partner in crime, the love of her life, her tough, resilient, sensitive, strong Bryce loved Thea back.

Thea could finally let herself believe it.

EPILOGUE

"I got an offer from Genevieve!"

Bryce had raced all the way to the bookstore to tell Thea. She'd found her with Mikey in the basement, setting up today's podcast. They'd started a new series, titled *Partners in Crime*: a chatty, fun, and less sinister turn on *Perfect Crimes*, where they told stories of survival volunteered by listeners — not just of murders and assault, but grief, graduations, marriages. A celebration of the way people could overcome things rather than paying homage to killers who didn't deserve their evil to be immortalized by fanatics with an affinity for the sick and twisted. They even had guest appearances from the likes of Thea's mother and Officer Shaw, and Bryce had told her own story here with Thea's encouragement.

It hadn't healed their wounds completely, and Bryce still felt sick when she thought of Peter and everything he'd put the people of Stone Grange through, but it was made easier each time she came here and remembered that they'd survived. And she had Thea now, in more ways than she ever had before. She was finding her happiness. Finally.

At the news, Thea gasped and jumped on Bryce without warning, ecstatic laughter bubbling in her chest. "My girl's going to have her very own documentary."

Bryce grinned wryly, face crinkling when Thea pressed a kiss to her cheek. "Well, she's not the only one."

"What do you mean?"

"I had Genevieve listen to our new episodes and she loved them. She wants the two of you working for her!"

"Are you kidding?" Shock cleaved its way across Mikey's features, and then crawled their way to Thea's too — but her smile didn't meet her eyes, and Bryce frowned.

"You don't want to?"

"Of course I do," tutted Thea. "But this is *your* opportunity, B. I don't want to take away from it."

"You're not taking away from it. You're sharing it with me." Just as they shared everything. Just as they always would. There was no one Bryce would rather do this with than Thea, and to tell her as much, she kissed her tenderly.

It earned a disgusted groan from Mikey. "Stop being all cute and in love in front of me."

"But we *are* cute and in love," Thea grinned, ruffling his hair, before turning back to Bryce. "What about Liv? They want you to travel for it, right?"

"There'll be breaks between filming." Despite her words, Bryce still chewed on her bottom lip nervously. It was something she'd gone over with her sister a million times already, almost emailing Genevieve to retract the offer a handful of times out of sheer worry that she was making a mistake. "I'll only be away two weeks at a time, and it's the summer after her graduation. I need to start trusting her to do the right thing — especially if she gets into Berkeley."

Liv was still waiting to hear back from the colleges she'd applied for, but of course Berkeley had been at the top of her list.

Thea squeezed Bryce's hands in reassurance. "My mom can watch out for her, too. She won't be alone."

But Bryce didn't think she'd need Thea's mother after all. Since the night of the drive-in, Liv had been much more responsible. Bryce had put it down to worry, since Liv had been terrified when Bryce had told her what had happened — even more so when she'd visited Thea in her hospital bed. Peter Keane was awaiting trial, on three counts of first degree murder and two counts of attempted murder; he was still recovering in the hospital. Bryce hadn't heard anything else of him since. She preferred it that way. Peter didn't deserve her time. He didn't deserve any of her.

Officer Shaw was still making her own recovery, with a few fractured ribs and a broken leg. She would testify at Peter's trial and had been lauded as the town's new hero. Bryce often saw her around in her booted walking cast and they always smiled and waved, though they didn't have much more to say to each other than that.

What had happened had changed everyone in Stone Grange, but not necessarily for the worst. Neighbors were friendlier. Even Gus had given Bryce paid leave from work those first few weeks after. What had happened had been awful and sickening, but it was survivable, and with plenty of counseling and community support, they'd all shown it.

Bryce and Thea had shown it.

"So we're doing this, team?" Mikey asked. It was the first time Bryce had seen him happy — really happy — since Hannah's death.

"We're doing this," Bryce grinned. It had been a long time since she'd felt this weightless, this *right,* and as they clutched hands and celebrated that morning with a new podcast episode, Bryce knew things were going to be okay.

She had her partners in crime by her side and a future to live. She had everything she needed — and she would never take it for granted.

ABOUT THE AUTHOR

Rachel Bowdler

Rachel Bowdler is a freelance writer, editor, and sometimes photographer from the UK. She spends most of her time away with the faeries. When she is not putting off writing by scrolling through Twitter and binge-watching sitcoms, you can find her walking her dog, painting, and passionately crying about her favorite fictional characters. You can find her on Twitter and Instagram @rach_bowdler.

BOOKS BY THIS AUTHOR

Paint Me Yours

The Flower Shop On Prinsengracht

The Divide

The Fate Of Us

Saving The Star

Dance With Me

Holding On To Bluebell Lodge

No Love Lost

Along For The Ride

The Secret Weapon

Printed in Great Britain
by Amazon

27102407R00081